Soul of Sin

Scandalous Scions Story 1.0

TRACY
COOPER-POSEY

STORIES RULE

EDMONTON • ALBERTA

Copyright © 2017 by Tracy Cooper-Posey
Text design by Tracy Cooper-Posey

Cover design by Dar Albert, Wicked Smart Designs
http://wickedsmartdesigns.com

Edited by Helen Woodall
http://helenwoodallfreelanceediting.blogspot.ca/

FIRST EDITION: June 2017

Cooper-Posey, Tracy
Soul of Sin/Tracy Cooper-Posey—1st Ed.

Romance—Fiction
Paranormal – Fiction

Praise for

Tracy Cooper-Posey's

historical romances

The main reason I ever began reading Cooper-Posey's work was her adventurous historical fiction - and she's back at it, in high style.

You will struggle to put it down. It is truly historical romance at its finest!

One of the better historical romances this reviewer has read in a long time.

Readers will be swept up into this stunning historical story.

Amazing amount of detail to the time period.

One of the best historical romances I have read this year. Tracy Cooper-Posey deftly blends historical detail with heart-touching romance.

The Great Family

Elisa and Vaughn Wardell

Marquess of Fairleigh, Viscount Rothmere

1825 Raymond, Viscount Marblethorpe (stepson)
1839 William Vaughn Wardell
1839 John (Jack) Gladwin Lochlann Mayes (fostered in 1846)
1842 Sarah Louise Wardell (D)
1843 Peter Lovell Wardell
1844 Gwendolyn (Jenny) Violet Moore Wardell (adopted in 1848)
1844 Patricia Sharla Victoria Mayes (fostered in 1846)
1849 Blanche Brigitte Colombe Bonnay (adopted in 1851)
1853 Emma Jane Wardell (adopted at birth)

Natasha and Seth Williams

Earl of Innesford, Baron Harrow (Ire.)

1839 Lillian Mary Harrow
1840 Richard Cian Seth Williams
1841 Neil Vaughn Williams
1843 Daniel Rhys Williams
1846 Bridget Bronte Williams & Mairin May Williams
1849 Annalies Grace Williams

Annalies and Rhys Davies

*Princess Annalies Benedickta of Saxe-Weiden, of the royal house Saxe
-Coburg-Weiden, Formerly of the Principality of Saxe-Weiden.*

1835 Benjamin Hedley Davies (adopted in 1845)
1842 Iefan William Davies
1843 Morgan Harrow Davies
1843 Sadie Hedley Davies (adopted in 1845)
1846 Bronwen Natasha Davies
1848 Alice Thomasina Davies (adopted at birth)
1849 Catrin Elise Davies

Chapter One

There was always a handful of people visiting West of London and Westminster Cemetery, every time Natasha returned there herself. If it were not for their black crepe and bombazine, it would be easy to lapse into thinking the visitors were strolling through a park, for the cemetery was garden-like in its appointments, with shady arbors, elaborate family crypts and well-clipped lawns.

No one spoke to anyone. That was the other difference. They were all strangers, there for a common purpose, yet still quite alone. Not even the civil nod of acknowledgement that strangers would exchange in Hyde Park was used here.

Natasha missed the path to the Innesford family crypt and lost her way. It had been so long since she had last visited, she could not remember how to find the building. Her discomfort rose.

When she found the crypt, her cheeks were hot with mortification and she was breathless from hurrying. She used the big iron key to unlock the gate and stepped into the cool, dim stillness of the hexagonal structure. Her boots crunched on the tiles, as grit shifted beneath her feet. It sounded loud in the small, marble-lined room and she flinched. She was disturbing the dead.

Seth was at the back, in the new wall. She slipped off her

glove and pressed her hand against the carved plate.

Richard Seth Williams
18th Earl of Innesford.
1804 A.D.—1854 A.D.

"Oh, Seth," she whispered, her eyes stinging with tears. "Three years since you were taken from me. It has been a year since I came to see you. I meant to come sooner. I miss you every day. I still forget sometimes that you are gone. I find myself starting to speak to you. Then I remember you are not there and it makes my chest ache."

There was no answer, of course. She wished for a moment she was spiritual enough to believe Seth watched over her and if she prayed hard enough and listened with a pure heart, he would speak to her. Other widows often claimed they had entire conversations with their departed husbands. They would consult with them on all major decisions in their life. The shades of their loved ones would continue to direct their lives from beyond the grave. It would be wonderful to be able to visit Seth eagerly and return to her life filled with the contentment and peace other widows derived from standing at the foot of their husbands' graves.

Instead, Natasha always stood here in the silence and felt confusion and a roil of emotions that all seemed wicked and inappropriate. Anger was one of the strongest. She sometimes wanted to beat her fist against the silent headstone and rage at the Fates for doing this to her and to Seth. Despair and grief and sadness were always there.

Yet more often, lately, what she felt was a terrible, fear-inducing loneliness.

Seth had been a pragmatic man. Seven years a convict had stripped from him any belief in divine justice and he would have laughed at those widows who talked to their dead husbands. Natasha, though, was beginning to understand why they might. It was comforting to think Seth might be lingering in some other plane and watching over her. Although if that *were* true, then Seth would be caustically advising her to give up such nonsensical ideas and go put on that blue dress he liked so much....

Her tears spilled. She hung her head.

"I don't know what to do," she whispered. "I'm so busy, Seth. There are never enough hours in the day. The twins are turning into ladies right in front of me. Lisa Grace is nine...*nine*, Seth. She is going to be tall. She is already up to my shoulder. And Daniel's voice has broken. He's a baritone. I know you would laugh about that. You'd have given him brandy to celebrate and perhaps a cigar. Neil is in his last year at Eton. Lilly..." She sighed. "Lilly seems content. Oh, and Cian starts at Cambridge this year. I decided...I hope you don't mind, but I thought he should finish his education, even though he's already taking over the management of his titles and the estates..."

She reached under the lace veil and wiped her cheeks. "Every time someone calls me the Dowager Countess, I look over my shoulder to see who it is they're addressing. Then I realize it is me they are talking to." She laid her hand back on the stone, her damp fingers marking it. "I don't feel like a dowager anything." She closed her eyes and leaned her head against the stone. "I just feel so *alone*."

The silence was her answer. No ghost whispered. Nor did the wind stir to shift leaves over the paths outside.

Natasha listened. She heard her heart beat and that was all. It was a strong beat. Healthy. She had turned forty years old in March yet she still felt as strong and alive as she had at twenty, when she had met Seth. She stayed silent when friends gently pointed out that as she was getting on in years, it was time to let go of the ribbons and frivolities of a younger woman and graciously linger in the darker corners of parlors. In the mirror, her face had not changed all that much. Her waist was only an inch wider after bearing seven children—thanks to daily walking and working in the garden, horse riding and energetic games of tennis with Annalies when no one was looking.

She was not an old woman, yet the world thought she should be. To dispute them would heap shame and scorn and notoriety upon her head. If Seth were still here, she might have had the courage to look everyone in the eye and do what she wanted. Only, Seth was no longer here to protect her.

Natasha sighed. "I suppose I must sort it out for myself. I always looked to you to help me understand matters. You were so good at understanding how people worked. You were forced to it by circumstances. Now I will have to do it for myself. I suppose these are my circumstances, aren't they?" She patted the inscription plate one more time. "I'll try to visit sooner, next time," she promised him.

She stepped out into the warm June morning, glad of the veil to hide her tear-stained cheeks. She locked the gate on the crypt, dropped the key into her reticule and moved slowly along the path. It seemed wrong that the sun was shining and the air held not a breath of chill. She could smell musky lavender and tea roses and the pleasant green smell of freshly cut grass. A bee buzzed past her veil. Doves twittered and cooed in the long arbor. Even here among the dead, the world was vitally alive.

On the path, ahead, a man was standing in front of a large, new headstone. The carved lettering on the black marble had been painted with gold leaf. He stood very still in front of it, his hands at his sides, his soft brimmed hat held in one of them. He was not speaking to the interred, as so many people did here.

The sun gleamed in his black hair as he turned his head at her approach.

Natasha had been on the point of apologizing for her intrusion, for this was the only way back to the gate of the cemetery, where her carriage was waiting. Then she realized she knew the man.

It was Raymond Devlin, Elisa's son.

Surprised skittered through her. "Lord Marblethorpe," she said and fell silent. All the usual polite social phrases seemed inappropriate in this place. All the family matters she might have asked about were just as wrong. She cast about for something to say.

"Countess Innesford," Raymond replied, with a small nod of acknowledgement. He glanced at the headstone he was standing before. A tiny frown grew between his dark brows.

"I interrupted you," Natasha said quickly. "I can find another—"

"I was about to leave, anyway," he said, just as quickly. "Let me see you back to your carriage."

Natasha pressed her lips together. She didn't want to deal with company right now. Only, standing awkwardly in the middle of the path was even more uncomfortable, so she nodded and moved down the footpath again.

Raymond fell in next to her. He didn't offer his elbow, which would have felt just as wrong. He didn't speak either, which was a relief to her. He settled his hat back in place and kept his gaze on his feet.

It was even more of a relief to move through the big stone arch and over to the waiting carriages. It put the other world behind her. The chitter of larks seemed natural and right once more. The clop of horses and whizz of carriage wheels on Brompton Road pulled her attention back to the normal day.

Raymond straightened and seemed to grow even taller. He glanced at her. "I do apologize for not conversing. It didn't seem right, to chat about the living, in there."

Natasha let out her breath. "Yes, exactly," she admitted. "You were...visiting Rose?" She surreptitiously wiped her cheeks dry, then lifted the veil up and pinned it to the back of her bonnet.

Raymond's dark-eyed gaze slid away from her. "It will be a year in August. I felt it would be delinquent to only visit on the anniversary, as if I had been neglecting her, I suppose." He rubbed the back of his neck awkwardly. "I thought if I visited sooner, then it would demonstrate I was not…a bad man."

His confession, so awkwardly admitted, let something inside her relax. "I wish I had thought of that," she said candidly. "I feel guilty because it has been a year since I last was here. I mean, I miss Seth. Dreadfully. Yet the days keep rolling past, faster and faster and then, suddenly, a year has gone by." It didn't seem wrong to speak of it to Raymond. He was Elisa's oldest son, a part of the greater family. He had seen Natasha romping on the croquet court. He had lost his wife, too. Also, he had known Seth.

Raymond drew in a breath that made his chest lift. "I know exactly what you mean," he said quietly. He glanced at the two carriages. "This might seem odd. May I send your carriage away and take you home in mine? I would like to talk."

"It doesn't seem odd at all," Natasha admitted. "Besides," she added. "We're family. Inside the family—"

"—we do as we please." He smiled. It was a small expression. "I will talk to your driver. Stay right there."

He strode down the petunia-lined path, his long boots gleaming as he moved. He stopped at Barny's side and spoke to him. Raymond was tall enough that he didn't have to strain to speak to him as Natasha would have. He merely raised his chin.

Barny tugged at his bowler brim, picked up the whip and tapped the back of the horses. The carriage moved off, sliding past Raymond's smart cabriolet. Raymond's driver soothed the gray with murmurs and clicks of his tongue.

Raymond opened the little door for her and held out his hand. Natasha gripped her crinolines with her right and took his hand with her left, then stepped up into the carriage. She made sure to sit as far to the left as she could, so Raymond would have room on the seat. She tucked the folds of gray and green plaid underneath her hip to make more room. These little cabriolets the younger men favored did not have the space of a full coach and four.

Raymond stepped up into the carriage, his weight making it dip to one side, the springs compressing. He paused, looking at the bench. She had taken up just over half of it with her skirts. She held them aside. "Twenty yards of plaid and linen. In my first season a dress with this much yardage would have been considered extravagant. Now, it is barely enough if one wants to be considered fashionable."

Raymond settled on the seat next to her and knocked on the roof. The gray stepped smartly forward, without jarring the carriage into motion. "Nevertheless, you have left me more than enough room," he said. "If my hips really are as wide as the bench you've supplied, I am badly in need of exercise."

Natasha could feel a smile pulling at her mouth. "I would advise filling in more dance cards, then. Three waltzes, back to back, will quickly reduce your waistline."

"And my wind," Raymond replied dryly. "Is that why you dance so often?"

"I like dancing," Natasha admitted. "I always have. I met

Seth at the Sweet Pea Ball…" She bit her lip.

Raymond looked at her, his brow lifting just a little. "Why do you stop?"

"I suppose…" She looked at her gloved hands, the chain of her reticule wrapped around the satin.

"We're family, remember?" Raymond said quietly. "Even though we're not related, we're closer than kin. You can speak your mind." His mouth lifted a little. "That will leave me free to speak mine, too."

Natasha hesitated, then plunged. "I shouldn't care to dance, anymore, only I do. I shouldn't care to do a great many things, now Seth has gone. I should care for nothing, I'm told. Yet I…still do." She let out a shaky breath.

Raymond nodded. "You're still young. Of course you still care about things."

She laughed. It was a weak sound. It was so odd hearing one of the children of the family dispense advice and opinions to one of the adults. "I'm not young by any definition, Raymond. I am your mother's friend. I watched you grow up."

"I am thirty-three," Raymond said, his voice low. "I won't presume to guess how old you are, Natasha, although I know you are not much older than I. You are my mother's friend, yes, but friendship crosses all barriers and years."

Natasha fell silent, confused by the strange tightness in her chest and the uncomfortable sensations it was creating. It was true. She was only seven years older than him. How had she not noticed that before? Was it because she had always separated the family into two distinct strata? The adults and the children and never the twain shall meet? Or had it been because Seth had been thirteen years older than her and she had elevated her perspective to match his?

"It is because of the closeness of our ages that I feel safe telling you what I am about to say," Raymond added.

Natasha rested her hand on his wrist, for a brief moment. "Are you about to tell me you didn't love Rose? I can save you the agony of confession, Raymond. It is a secret only to a very few of the family anymore."

Raymond hesitated. "I have never hidden that the marriage was purely one of duty to me," he said evenly. "My father's family insisted. I could put it off no longer. I complied. The Devlin family have their heir. I have done my duty." He shrugged.

The harshness of his voice, the inflexibility of his jaw, surprised her. The depth of his feelings were also shocking. "You are angry," she said. "I'm sorry, that was not my intention, to make you angry."

He shook his head, frowning. "I am not angry at you. If I am angry at all, it is at myself, for…oh, all manner of things. I didn't love Rose. It has been nearly a year and yet this morning, I still looked up expecting to see her sitting at the other end of the breakfast table, buttering her toast." His gloved hand curled into a hard fist. "Why do I keep doing that?" He ground out the question, pain in his voice.

"You may not have loved her in the way you think you ought to have, but there was affection there, Raymond. Respect, at the very least, or you would not have made an heir. You are not the sort to…to…" Natasha took a deep breath.

"You are not the sort of man to bed a woman with whom you have no relationship whatsoever. I do not believe that is in your nature. You cared for Rose on some level and you lived with her for five years—"

"Four," he corrected softly.

"It was long enough for the relationship to leave its mark on your heart, Raymond."

"Then why do I feel guilty all the time?" he asked flatly. "I feel guilty for not loving her enough, for not giving her all the affection I could. If I had known she would live so few years, I would have…" He shook his head.

Natasha jumped. Guilt. Yes, that was it. That was the ache in the middle of her chest. "I don't think it matters what the type or quality the relationship may have been," she said slowly. "What matters is that they have gone and we remain and we feel guilty for it."

Raymond considered her, his gaze steady. The pain in his eyes faded. "Yes," he said. "That's it, exactly." He sat back in the corner, almost relaxing into it. "We are a wretched pair, are we not?"

The air of free confession still lingered, which allowed Natasha to say, "I do not feel as wretched as I should, knowing someone else feels as I do."

Raymond didn't move or speak for a long moment. The carriage rounded the long curve into Knightsbridge. The tall trees of Hyde Park were visible over the buildings lining the wide road. They would be in Mayfair soon enough.

"My marriage was doomed from the start," Raymond said. "I knew that, yet I married her anyway." His gaze shifted from Natasha's. "I loved someone else. I think I have loved her forever."

Natasha nodded.

"You knew?" he asked, shock making his voice rise.

"Not for certain. Everyone has wondered for years if there was a woman you could not speak of. You never seemed to get into mischief the way Benjamin does, or that other single men are supposed to." Natasha hesitated, then threw caution away. This frankness was helping ease aches and torments that had lived in her for a long time. It must surely be helping Raymond, too. "Did she…is the woman you love still unavailable, Raymond? I mean, you are a widower. It has been nearly a year. You are free to pursue whomever you wish, now."

"If the woman would have me," Raymond said in agreement. "Her name is Susanna."

Natasha cast about quickly, names of friends and relatives, the peerage of England and Scotland and Ireland running through her head. She didn't know a Susanna. "Is she…a commoner? Is that why you've never spoken of her before?"

He weighed his answer. Then he shook his head. "I can say no more. It would not be fair to her. It may even compromise her position."

The woman he loved, this Susanna, was married. Perhaps even happily married. Natasha could read between the lines as well as any other society matron navigating the twin shoals of finding a good match for her daughters and warding off inappropriate matches for her sons. Marriages arranged with an eye toward securing titles and lands, with no regard for love and affection, were not unusual, alas. Yet society still maintained the pretense that every marriage was a love match. Raymond's Susanna, if she was of the peerage, may have been forced to such a match by family pressure, just as Raymond had been forced to his.

Raymond must have lingered for years, saying nothing, perhaps waiting for Susanna, who was then wed to another. After that, he had refused to consider anyone else, until his father's family had insisted upon an heir, at which point, Raymond had acquiesced and married Rose.

Natasha studied him, seeing him in this new light. He had always been a silent, introspective man. Now she knew why. "I'm glad you told me this much," she said impulsively.

Raymond lifted his hand, in a small gesture of caution. "I should not have spoken at all," he said. "I only wanted you to know I understand. You loved Seth very much. I saw it when he was alive and I know how you feel now, because I, too, can't be with the one I love."

Her heart shifted. "Oh, Raymond…"

"In the last year," he went on, "I have learned that speaking my mind, that saying what is truly in my heart to a sympathetic listener, can ease the load."

"You have done that for me, this morning," Natasha admitted. "I was utterly miserable, until we spoke."

His mouth turned up at the corners. Warmth lit his eyes. "I am glad of that," he said softly. He glanced over her shoulder. "Piccadilly. We'll be there in a moment or two." He sat up again and spoke of general things—the upcoming

Henley Regatta of which he was a marshal this year, which was considered a great honor; of the racing at Ascot; and of family things, such as Annalies' daughter, Sadie, and her latest ambition to join a circus when she grew up. It was delightful chatter, filled with people they had in common, which were many. Natasha felt relaxed and very nearly happy when the cabriolet eased to a stop outside the townhouse on Park Lane.

Raymond stepped onto the pavement and turned to hand her out of the carriage.

Natasha gripped his hand a little longer than was strictly necessary. "Thank you, Raymond. You truly have eased my heart a little."

His fingers pressed hers, then he let her hand go and stepped back, as was proper. "I, too, am glad we spoke." His eyes met hers.

Natasha dropped her gaze, aware of passers-by observing them. "I would ask you in, only there is no one at home. Besides," she added hurriedly, "I have to take tea this afternoon at the London Orphans Society. There is a perfectly dreadful woman from Scotland who is to lecture us on how to raise money."

Raymond smiled. "Did your Orphans Society not raise nearly ten thousand pounds last year?" he asked curiously.

"Yes!" Natasha said heatedly. "Yet now we are to be told we are not doing it properly."

"The cheek of her!" Raymond said. Only, his shoulders were shaking. He was laughing and hiding it.

Natasha realized how shrill and silly she sounded and

smiled, too. "I was thinking I may send a letter to your mother and insist she invited me for afternoon tea *before* I received the invitation from the Society. Then I would simply have to decline the later invitation."

Raymond gave her a short bow. "Far be it for me to get in the way of social machinations. Good day, Lady Innesford."

"Lord Marblethorpe." She picked up her hems. Corcoran was already standing at the door, waiting for her to enter. She slipped inside and heard the cabriolet roll away from the door as Corcoran closed it.

"Was that Viscount Marblethorpe, my lady?" he asked.

"It was," Natasha said as she took off the veil and bonnet and dropped the hat pin inside. She handed it over to her maid, Mulloy, along with her gloves and the light shawl that was all that was needed in June. "Raymond was at the cemetery, too."

"Visiting his poor wife," Corcoran guessed. "Such a tragedy. Lunch will be ready in the dining room at the hour, my lady."

She glanced at the grandfather clock ticking heavily in the corner of the front hall. Noon was barely fifty minutes away. "I need to send a letter to Lady Farleigh, Corcoran. Can Kip run the letter over to Grosvenor Square for me?"

"Certainly, my lady. I'll stir the lad up from the kitchen for you."

"Mulloy, would you set out my afternoon dress? I'll be up as soon as I've written the letter."

"Yes, my lady." Mulloy curtsied and hurried upstairs

with Natasha's things.

Natasha went through to the library, where her desk was located. It had been Seth's desk, of course. Now it was hers. It would be Cian's soon enough. He could claim his full inheritance this very day if he chose to. It was his by right. He was as reluctant, though, to take up his father's mantle as Natasha had been for him to do so.

She had resisted using the desk up until now. Usually, she used the lap secretary, even going so far as to sit at the dining table instead of here.

Now she sat down and pulled out stationery from the central drawer and barely thought of the fact that Seth used to sit here, swearing over pilfering fingers and cargoes that were short, rotting or spoiled from sea water, or that reliable staff for Harrow Hall in Ireland were difficult to find from his desk in London. He would grumble, but stay in London for the Season to make friends of the right people, just so their children would have the best opportunities when they came of age.

She rested her hand on the leather inlay for a moment and realized she was smiling. Seth would have been just as happy as her to wriggle out of an unpleasant social engagement as she was doing now.

Still smiling, she wrote her letter to Elisa. The afternoon suddenly seemed brighter.

Chapter Two

Natasha looked over her cards and sighed. Whist was not her favorite game, especially if Annalies was playing it with her. Annalies seemed to be able to remember every card that had been played. Her brain must turn mechanically. Natasha never failed to lose—quite badly—when Annalies and Elisa were at the table. Even Lilly, their fourth player, was playing better than Natasha, even though she was distracted and kept cleaning her spectacles.

"Are the children being a bother this afternoon, Lilly?" Natasha asked her daughter kindly.

Lilly looked startled. "No, not at all!" She glanced at Elisa apologetically. "I assigned *The Lady of Shalott* for reading this afternoon. It is too warm for more energetic studies."

It was *very* warm. The drapes at the tall windows had been drawn back as far as possible and the windows opened wide. There was not a hint of a breeze. The scent of dry dust from the road outside the windows was strong and made stronger each time a horse or carriage passed, which was not often, for all of London seemed to have fallen into a stupor this afternoon.

"I do so like *The Lady of Shalott*," Annalies said. "If the girls enjoy it as much as I do, that explains why it is quiet upstairs." She was not frowning over her cards as everyone else did. She waited, her cards in her lap.

"Floating down a shady river does seem rather attractive right now," Elisa murmured, rearranging her cards. "For June, it is unseasonably hot." She fanned her face with her cards, lifting the white gold curls from her temples.

"I've kept you from cooler pursuits, haven't I?" Natasha said, guilt spearing her.

"Nonsense," Elisa said firmly. "Rescuing a friend from social purgatory always comes first."

"Absolutely," Annalies said, just as firmly. "Is this Scottish woman really as dreadful as you say? Perhaps she does have some notions that would help with the Society?"

"You are always looking for new and better ways to do things, Anna," Elisa told her. "The people whom Natasha must coax to part with their money for a worthy cause are far more staid. Tradition and custom serve better."

"There, that is precisely what I told the President when she suggested the lecture," Natasha said.

Annalies sat back with a sigh. "I cannot concentrate," she declared. "This heat is pickling my mind inside my skull. Much more of it and vinegar will run from my ears."

Natasha laughed at the notion.

Elisa threw down her cards. "I agree. It is more than uncomfortable."

"That is because you have the windows open," Natasha told her, folding her hand, too.

Elisa and Annalies both groaned.

"Not the window thing again, please!" Elisa said. "Seth would never stop..." she glanced at Natasha, "*lecturing* about the windows."

"Well, it *is* very hot in Australia. Hotter than even today, I imagine," Natasha said.

Lilly lurched to her feet. Her face was pale. "I am...I want to see to the girls, make sure they're behaving themselves." She hurried away, scattering cards as she went, and flashing ankles as she dashed up the stairs.

Paulson, the butler, who was just entering, bent to pick up the cards with a bellow of breath. His knees were not what they had once been.

Elisa watched Lilly leave. She looked at Natasha. "I am so sorry. That was thoughtless of me, to bring up his name like that."

Natasha pressed her hand over Elisa's. "Lilly is sensitive about her father's death. Far more than anyone else. She'll adjust eventually. She just needs time."

Elisa didn't seem convinced. She pressed her lips together.

Annalies was the one to speak, though. "We all miss him, of course. You mustn't think we don't."

"Of course I don't think that!" Natasha declared, shocked.

"It's just that Raymond warned us where you had been this morning and you were...upset," Elisa said gently. "I suppose Seth is on all our minds right now."

Natasha could feel the sting of tears and blinked rapidly. She waited until the hard knot in her throat dissipated, then said calmly, "Is that why you were suddenly free this afternoon? Because Raymond told you I would ask to be invited?"

Elisa gave a tiny shrug. "Even if he had not sent his note, a gap in my schedule would have mysteriously appeared when you asked, anyway."

"Mine, too," Annalies said.

Natasha smiled at them. "Thank you. Both of you."

Annalies handed the rest of the card pack to Paulson as he came over to the table. He put the section together with his stack and placed the full deck back on the table. "I thought you might enjoy tea under the willow tree, my lady," he said to Elisa. "There is the tiniest of breezes out in the garden at the moment."

"That seems like an excellent idea, Paulson, thank you," Elisa said and got to her feet. "Could you ask the maids to close all the windows and draw all the drapes in the house, please?"

Natasha smiled.

"My lady?" Paulson stared at her as if she had barked like a dog.

"Yes, I want the whole house closed up tight so no more heat can get in. Around sunset, we will open the house up again and let the cooler air circulate until it is time to retire."

Paulson was as devoted to Elisa and her family as Corcoran was to Seth's family, yet Elisa often stretched the limits of his devotion, as she was doing now. Annalies and Natasha watched him struggle, until he finally cleared his throat and gave a stiff nod. "Very well, my lady."

As they moved out to the terrace, to where the table and chairs had been set out under the shade of the century old willow tree, Natasha murmured; "He will assume it was all his own idea once he realizes how effective it is at cutting down the heat."

"If it *does* reduce this heat, Paulson can claim himself Emperor and I will not care," Elisa said, plucking away the edge of her afternoon dress from her chest.

"If it is still this hot in October, then I really am going to swim in the ocean this year," Annalies added.

Natasha laughed. Annalies had been threatening to swim in public for many years. The waves and the beach fascinated her. "Then you will be arrested and the family will add one more scandal to its repertoire."

"You've never gone swimming in the sea, have you, Natasha?" Elisa asked, as they sat at the table. "All those years in Cornwall, listening to the waves, you were never tempted?"

Natasha picked up the teapot and poured, even though Elisa had not asked her to.

"She has!" Annalies breathed. "When?"

Natasha could feel her cheeks burning. "With Seth, one night…oh, a very long time ago." She held out the cup to Elisa and stared at her, daring her to comment about inappropriate behavior.

Elisa took the cup and smiled. "Happy memories," she said, making Natasha wonder what outdoor water sport Elisa may have indulged in.

Annalies leaned forward. "Were you…did you take off your clothes? All of them?" she asked, her tone intensely curious.

Natasha sought for a way to shift the conversation. Then she remembered. "Elisa, has Raymond ever spoken to you about a woman called Susanna?"

Elisa sat back, her expression thoughtful. "Susanna? Not that I recall. That isn't to say he doesn't know a woman called Susanna. Raymond has always been very discreet about his affairs."

"That is because he didn't have any," Natasha told her. "Except for Susanna."

"An *affaire de coer*?" Annalies asked. "Who is she?"

"I don't know," Natasha said. "Raymond wouldn't tell me. He was…" She hesitated. "He was trying to cheer me up, so he told me about her and that she was the great love of his life."

Elisa's lips parted and her eyes widened.

"You didn't know?" Annalies asked her.

"No," Elisa said, a small furrow forming between her brows. "How odd. I mean…" She glanced at Natasha and Anna self-consciously. "It is quite normal for a man to keep his dalliances away from his mother's attention, but the love of his life?" She shook her head.

Annalies was sitting with her teacup halfway to her mouth, her gaze distant. Her lips moved, while she made no sound.

"What are you doing, Anna?" Natasha asked curiously.

"I am reviewing *Burke's*," Annalies said distantly.

It was only the three of them and the greater family to whom Annalies revealed her ability to memorize and recall whole books of information. The rest of society already considered the Queen's cousin to be a very odd duck and such parlor tricks would have been viewed doubtfully.

Natasha and Elisa, though, were used to Anna's gaze growing unfocused for sometimes minutes at a time. Then she would refocus and recite a quote or a fact or a figure that would halt even the most strenuous argument in its tracks.

Natasha had stopped bothering to check the facts in the actual book at a later time. Anna was never wrong. She turned to Elisa instead. "I think Raymond has never spoken of the woman before now because she is in some way completely unavailable to him. After Rose, now he is recovering, he is speaking of her because it will help him to move on."

"You seem to have had quite the conversation with him, this morning," Elisa said.

Natasha put her cup down. "He was very sweet, Elisa. We were both down. It was good to talk."

"You know you can speak to me and Annalies about anything, don't you?" Elisa said anxiously.

"Of course," Natasha assured her.

"Even Rhys and Vaughn, if you need a man's perspective."

"I know," Natasha replied.

Elisa relaxed. "Well, then," she said awkwardly. Direct conversations about highly personal and delicate issues did not come easily to her.

Natasha picked up the cake slice. "Gingerbread, anyone?"

Annalies put her cup on the table. "Yes, please," she

declared. "Two, if I may." She never gained any inches, no matter how much she ate.

"Did you find Susanna in the *Peerage*?" Elisa asked.

Annalies shook her head. "No Susanna. Although she could be just about anywhere, in these modern days of travel. Eastern Europe. *Burke's Peerage* doesn't include Balkan royalty."

"Or maybe she is a commoner," Natasha pointed out, surprised that Annalies, who had married a commoner herself, had not thought of it.

Annalies nodded, taking her first plate of gingerbread. "Yes, of course. She could easily be a commoner." She glanced at Elisa. "One of the daughters of those very rich northern families that run all the factories, perhaps."

Elisa didn't respond to the teasing. "Surely it doesn't matter who she is? She has gone from Raymond's life. I applaud him for trying to move on."

Natasha put the second plate in front of Elisa. "Of course it matters, to you."

Elisa sighed. "Hang it all, yes."

* * * * *

The Devlin family home on Berkeley Square was a tall, white upright structure built in austere Georgian fashion. Although Elisa had never told Raymond, she considered the house to be quite ugly.

Raymond, though, enjoyed his independence. He would have been most welcome to return to their family home—

Vaughn had extended the offer more than once. If Raymond had accepted the offer, then Elisa could have helped him with the care of his son.

She understood, though, why Raymond had gently refused to return to the Wardell residences...or at least she thought she had understood up until Natasha's startling revelation yesterday that Raymond had carried a secret love for a very long time.

Natasha had asked Elisa not to pursue the matter, yet after a sleepless night of restlessly turning and tangling bedsheets and disturbing Vaughn, who normally slept as soundly as a hibernating bear, Elisa realized she simply could not let it be.

Thomsett, Raymond's young butler, opened the door quickly for her. "Lady Farleigh," he said in his quiet, well-spoken voice. "This is a pleasure. I am sure Lord Raymond will be very happy to see you." His green eyes were warm and welcoming.

"I do apologize for arriving without warning in this way," Elisa told him, as she happily removed her gloves and bonnet. "Raymond is at home?"

"He has a guest at the moment, although I do believe the gentleman intends to leave at any moment. I was about to take his hat and cane through."

Thomsett gave off the air of someone managing a flurry of unexpected activity with aplomb and grace that didn't match his youth. He had begun service with Raymond only a few years ago. Elisa did not know anything about him, although she assumed that Raymond had looked into his references properly before hiring him. The one thing Elisa did know about the butler was that at some time in the past, he had been in the military. He had the upright bearing and square shouldered stance that only came from a military officer's career.

Thomsett, though, was as discreet as Paulson.

"Ah, there we," Thomsett murmured, as male voices grew louder, issuing from the library.

Two men stepped into the hall, both of them halting when they saw Elisa.

"Good morning, Mother," Raymond said, barely looking surprised.

The other man was Benjamin Hedley, Anna and Rhys' adopted son. He smiled with delight when he saw her. "Aunt Elisa, what a surprise!" He kissed her cheek, his full black beard and moustache tickling her. Both were neatly trimmed, with none of the curled and waxed ends some men adopted. He had coal black eyes that matched his hair and porcelain white flesh. His Welsh heritage was quite evident.

His very white teeth flashed beneath his moustache and his eyes twinkled. "You are just in time, Aunt Elisa. Please talk this fellow into helping out his old team in July. We're short a man thanks to a posting to India."

"I've already explained I am to be one of the marshals," Raymond said. "As much as I would like to help out."

Benjamin rolled his eyes. "He's being a stick in the mud."

"I believe Raymond is only insisting upon doing what he

has first promised to someone else. Could Will or Jack help out, instead?" Elisa said, freely offering either of her oldest sons.

"Jack doesn't row and Will is already in the team." Benjamin sighed as he took his hat and cane from Thomsett. "I suppose I could ask one of the fellows at the club."

"There's the ticket," Raymond said.

Benjamin strode out of the house, not looking too upset at Raymond's refusal.

"Is it very bad to lose a man so close to the Regatta?" Elisa asked Raymond as Thomsett closed the door.

"Benjamin is making far too much of it in his usual fashion," Raymond said easily. "It is nearly a fortnight until the Regatta. He'll spend a lot of time beating his chest about the loss, so everyone will feel sorry for him. Then he'll ask Percy at the club and Percy will ask him why it took that long to ask."

Elisa laughed.

Even Thomsett smiled. "Fresh tea, my lord?"

"Is there any of that lemonade Mrs. Fraser made yesterday?" Raymond asked.

"I'm sure we can scare some up," Thompsett said and headed to the back of the house.

Raymond moved toward the library once more. "Come in, Mother."

"Could we use the morning room instead? The library is so dark and dreary," Elisa said.

Raymond froze for one small moment. "Of course," he said shortly and crossed the hall to the opposite door.

"Although I haven't been in here for a while, so I have no idea what the state of the room is…" He paused inside the door, looking around.

Elisa stopped by his shoulder.

"Exactly the same," Raymond muttered.

Elisa patted his arm. "Yet not quite the same, I'm sure. It's time to put it to different uses, don't you think?" She moved around him and over to the French parlor sofa sitting by the fire and picked up all the cushions and put them in the wing chair next to it. "There's absolutely no need to hunch up next to the fire at this time of year. This sofa would be better placed with the sideboard behind it. Could you ask Thomsett and a footman to arrange it?"

Raymond looked at her steadily for a moment. Then he went over to the bell pull and tugged on it. One of the footmen appeared swiftly and Raymond explained what needed doing.

The man hurried away, then returned a few minutes later with Thomsett and another footman.

Raymond raised a brow. "Mother?" he asked pointedly.

Elisa had taken the few moments of waiting to sort out the seating in her mind. She gave directions on where the furniture was to be moved, then stepped over to the door with Raymond, well out of the way.

Two maids and another footman had also been called in to help, by the time the room was rearranged to Elisa's satisfaction. The new arrangement made the most of the view through the three windows, overlooking the square and the shady trees there. The sideboard, that had lived up against the wall, now sat behind the sofa, its pleasing lines facing the door. The bowl of roses was placed on the sideboard, where guests would see them as soon as they entered.

"It looks strange," Raymond complained.

"It is French," Elisa said. "You'll learn to like it, trust me."

He bent over the bowl of pink blooms. "These are fresh." He sounded surprised.

"The maids will have cut fresh flowers and placed them here every few days, whether you saw them or not," Elisa assured him.

He looked at her, startled. "Why would they do that?"

"Because you are not the only one to miss Rose," she said gently.

He snapped upright and moved to the wing chair, which was now opposite the sofa, its back to the fireplace. Both chair and sofa were sitting in the light coming through the windows. Raymond settled himself in the chair and looked around. "Very strange," he muttered.

Thomsett came in with a tray bearing the lemonade jug and glasses. "There was even a little ice left, my lord," he added as he placed the tray on the table beside Raymond. The ice tinkled against the side of the jug.

Elisa's throat contracted longingly at the sound. "Perhaps, if there is any more lemonade left, Thomsett, you and the staff should have it after all your efforts just now. Raymond?"

"Yes, please help yourself," Raymond said without hesitation.

Thomsett smiled. "It will be most welcome, my lord, Lady Farleigh. Thank you."

"I'll see to the drinks," Raymond told him. "You go and have yours."

"Thank you, my lord."

Elisa waited until Thomsett had closed the door. "Where *did* you find Thomsett, Raymond? He seems far too young to be so…old."

"Competent is the word you are looking for, I believe." Raymond poured two glasses of lemonade, dropped sugar lumps into hers along with a spoon and passed her the glass. "A fellow I knew at Cambridge who went into the Army recommended Thomsett to me. Blackwood—"

"The Marquess of Ladbroke?" Elisa asked, for she knew the family.

"Cory Blackwood is the second son," Raymond said.

"He bought a commission?"

"No, actually. He always knew he was heading for the military. He didn't like the idea of buying himself rank and privilege. He graduated from the Royal Military Academy at Woolwich and went into the Artillery. He's a Colonel now. He was caught up in the mutiny in India."

"Thomsett, too?" Elisa asked.

"No, Thomsett was forced to retire for medical reasons, after the Crimean War."

"Retire? He's so young!"

Raymond nodded. "He was awarded a Victoria Cross."

"No!"

"He keeps it in the back of drawer somewhere."

"Surely, such a man could find a more challenging occupation, one better suited to his valor?"

"He likes the peace," Raymond said. "Butler to this household is challenge enough, he says." He shook his head. "He doesn't speak of it, but I believe Thomsett returned from Russia with demons eating his soul. It happens, in the military, especially for those in the very thick of the fighting."

Elisa sipped her lemonade, reconsidering Thomsett in this new light.

"And what brings you to my door this morning, Mother?" Raymond asked.

She put her glass aside. "Natasha told me a very strange story yesterday, about you."

"I saw her at the cemetery," Raymond said easily. "What story is that?"

"About a woman called Susanna." Elisa paused expectantly.

Raymond didn't react. He didn't move at all, or show any emotion. His face might have been carved from marble.

"Natasha was worried. You mustn't mind her telling me," Elisa added.

"Worried?" Raymond repeated woodenly.

"Who is she, this Susanna?" Elisa asked. "I know of no one by that name. Is she a commoner, Raymond? Is that why you feel you cannot—"

"Mother, stop," he said, his voice deepening. "Do you think, if I have not spoken of her in all these years, I would suddenly tell you everything at the first urging?

Elisa bit her lip. "No," she admitted reluctantly. "I suppose not. But surely—"

"No," he said firmly. "I cannot and will not say anything further about her. It would compromise her position. It would embarrass her and it would be of no use beyond either of those things."

Elisa stared at him, surprised. Raymond had never spoken so shortly with her before. It felt a little as though a normally placid dog had snapped at her without warning. Then Natasha had spoken truly. This secret woman really had snared his heart. "Did she trifle with you, Raymond?" Elisa asked, her heart aching for his. "Did she extend hope, to leave you dangling in this way?"

Raymond surged to his feet. "No. Never. She is and always has been a complete lady." He moved restlessly to the window and back, to grip the wing of the chair. He was not enjoying the conversation, yet he would not end it because he was her son.

Elisa spared him. She rose to her feet. "I must go," she said and pretended she did not see the relief in his face.

"Very well. I'll have Thomsett bring your things." He went over to the bell and tugged on it.

Elisa moved through to the front hall. When Raymond followed her, she turned to him and spoke quickly, before Thomsett arrived. "I know you are trying, but you must find a way to let her go, Raymond. You have ruined the first half of your life over a shadow and a thought, for that is all she really is, whoever she is. You deserve more."

Thomsett silently appeared with her gloves and bonnet.

Raymond tried to smile. It wouldn't form properly. "I will heed what you say," he told her, as she slid her gloves on and tied her bonnet.

Elisa was satisfied with that. "You're a good man, Raymond," she told him and reached up on tiptoe to kiss his cheek. "I'm also very glad you choose to shave!"

She was pleased to hear his soft chuckle as she left.

Chapter Three

The belting heat of late June faded as July whispered in with cooler breezes and a little rain to rescue parched gardens. It was still warm and bright and on cloudless days wandering the banks of the Thames was a very pleasant affair. Natasha was still completely grateful for the airiness and lightness of muslin and the shade of her parasol, as she perched on a stool, her skirts billowing out around her, and watched the activity on the river and in the enclosure, where most the *ton* was invited to spectate.

Natasha was not the only woman in white muslin. There was all manner of dresses on display. Flounced skirts, skirts draped up and pinned with fresh flowers. Dresses with insets, dresses with bell sleeves. Lady Rylstone wore muslin so thin, her corset cover showed as a pale ghost beneath. However, the embroidered, colorful flowers on the hem of her dress and over the bust distracted the eye.

There was as much cotton lace as there was muslin, plus ribbons and bows and pearl buttons. There were a hundred more parasols bobbing about the enclosure, too. It was all very pretty and enticing.

The men were also dressed as coolly as possible, with thin shirts and unbuttoned jackets and the lightest of cravats. She did not look closely enough to determine if any of them had dispensed with their undershirts, but would not be surprised if they had. Most of the jackets were striped, short sportsman jackets, although even the frockcoats on display were all pale colored fabrics, designed to reflect the heat.

There was a small breeze that rippled across the water, sending welcome moist air over the enclosure, although there was not as much water for it to fan across as there might have been, because of all the boats. There were dinghies and rowboats, rafts and more—anything that could float and carry passengers had been pressed into service, allowing spectators to get that much closer to the racing.

The little steam-driven cabin boat that officiated the finish line of the races was puttering across the river now, settling into position. Between races, the officials spent their time trying to herd the spectator craft out of the way of the race course.

Natasha looked around for Annalies and Elisa. They had left shortly after the last race to use the conveniences. They would be back shortly and the next race was about to begin. Rhys and Vaughn were in the shady corner where the brandy was in good supply. It left Natasha alone. She didn't mind. It was distracting, watching everyone wander the enclosure, or risk themselves on a wobbling boat. Most of the people here she knew, some very well and some by name only. Everyone who passed by knew her, too.

Far down the river, Natasha heard the pistol fire to mark the start of the next race. She looked around once more for Anna and Elisa and saw them coming toward her with a dark-haired woman between them. The woman was wearing muslin, too. There was a tartan cummerbund about her exceedingly slender waist.

Natasha's heart sank. This had to be the Scottish woman whom the London Orphans Society valued so highly. Anna and Elisa must have been introduced to her by someone— probably Lady Gaddesby, the President of the Society, who knew that Anna and Elisa were Natasha's closest friends. Lady Gaddesby had most likely urged Elisa to bring the woman to Natasha and introduce them. Elisa, always sensitive to public opinion and propriety, far more than Anna and Natasha were, would have obliged without demur.

Now here the woman was. Natasha cast about for her name. It had been supplied in the monthly newsletter from the Society, but she had quite forgotten it. Some Baronet from the Highlands…

"Lady Innesford," Elisa said, as they reached Natasha. "May I present to you a recent acquaintance? Morven, Lady Tachbrook of Scotland."

Natasha nodded at her. "Charmed, I'm sure," she said stiffly.

Lady Tachbrook's blue eyes met hers, as Elisa completed the introduction; "Lady Tachbrook, this is Lady Natasha, Countess of Innesford, Baroness Harrow."

Lady Tachbrook nodded her head. It was a gracious inclination that displayed the masses of black curls pinned up at the back of her head. "It is a great pleasure to meet you, Lady Innesford," she said. There was no hint of brogue in her voice and she had a lovely lilting way of speaking. "I have heard for many years about how beautiful you were. I see now that the gossip was accurate, for a change."

Natasha stared at her, startled. "I…er…thank you," she said inadequately. "How is it we've not met before now? I thought I knew everyone."

"I have been secluded near Inverness for many years," Lady Tachbrook replied. "I lost my husband when I was young. I heard of your husband's passing, too. I am very sorry."

Natasha drew in a breath and held it, keeping her reaction to the mention of Seth hidden. Then she relaxed and exhaled. "Thank you."

Elisa rested her hand on Natasha's shoulder for a moment. "Lady Gaddesby, who just introduced Lady Tachbrook to the Princess and I, wanted you to know that Lady Tachbrook has occupied herself with good deeds and charity work recently." Elisa's mouth turned down in a tiny grimace. She was acknowledging her regret for forcing Natasha to meet the woman.

Lady Tachbrook also wrinkled her nose. "Really, if you do not mind, call me Morven. I feel I must apologize for Lady Gaddesby's enthusiasm. She has thrust me upon society, because of some small successes I had building a fund for children in Inverness. She is rather…" Lady Tachbrook hesitated.

"Insistent?" Elisa suggested delicately.

"Bulldogs wilt before Mary Gaddesby," Annalies said, speaking in a voice that was not meant to carry.

Natasha felt her eyes widen. So did Lady Tachbrook's.

Suddenly, all four of them were laughing.

One of the enclosure staff brought over a fourth stool at

Elisa's gesture. The three women sat down to watch the race, for the competitors were coming into view. Lady Tachbrook—Morven—took the stool on Natasha's left and arranged her hems so the merest tip of her shoe showed beneath.

Natasha glanced at the woman. She had not a single thread out of place. Her dress was modest, becoming and completely appropriate for a woman her age, which appeared to be close to Natasha's. There was nothing about the woman that Natasha could criticize or dismiss.

Add to that her charming apology for the Orphan Society event and it was hard to maintain the dislike Natasha had formed based purely on the lady's reputation as put forth by Lady Gaddesby.

Everyone in the enclosure, including Morven, was staring at the river, watching the rowers fight it out for the lead. Shouts of encouragement and cheers sounded, although the volume was a mere racket now. As the race drew to the finish it would become deafening.

Natasha took the moment of distraction to lean closer to Annalies and murmur, *"Burke's?"*

Annalies didn't look at her. She kept her gaze on the river, instead, and clapped her encouragement. Underneath her clapping, she murmured, "Morven Annette Fortescue, wife of Baronet Tachbrook. He died twenty-one years ago. No heir."

Natasha turned her gaze to the river once more. So, Morven Fortescue had been widowed a very long time.

The shouting and cries from the spectators in the enclosure shifted to notes of alarm and dismay. Natasha got to her feet, her attention turned fully upon the race.

One of the spectator craft had floated out too far into the middle of the river. The racing team heading toward them had their backs to the prow of their boat and had no idea there was an obstruction on the course. The women in the drifting dinghy were standing up, screaming in panic, while the men tried to paddle out of the way with their hands and a third reached uselessly for the drifting oars.

The sound the crowd was making was one of combined warning and alarm. Surely the racing crew could hear them?

Natasha drew in a sharp breath as the narrow nose of the racing boat slammed into the dinghy, with a crunch and splinter of wood. The dinghy shivered in the water and everyone in it was jolted backwards. One of the women windmilled her arms and screamed as she toppled back into the water with a loud splash. Natasha thought it might be Lady Emily Dacre, the youngest daughter of Viscount Dacre.

Her companion was a gentleman. He tore off his jacket and instantly dived into the water after her.

The racing crew's boat was sinking. Oars floated everywhere and three of the four-man crew were already in the water. The fourth gripped the gunwales of the dinghy, trying heroically to prevent it from floating farther out into the river, into the path of the other rowing teams. The dinghy was far heavier than he, though, and the river flowed strongly here. He was pulled from the sinking row boat and was forced to let the dinghy go to save himself.

A second competing boat rammed into the dinghy, tossing another passenger, a man, into the river. It also collided with the oar of the fourth crewman from the first boat. As he was still holding onto the oar, it pushed him into the water with a yell.

Everyone watching fell silent, waiting for everyone to surface.

Heads popped back up. Natasha counted quickly. Everyone was there, including the fourth oarsman. They all began swimming for the shore and the crowd clapped and cheered, relieved that no one was injured. There was some laughter spattered among the clapping. A moment's entertainment in amongst the races was always appreciated.

Many hands reached out to help the swimmers back onto shore. They stepped onto the banks, streaming water and smiling, mostly.

"They're coming this way," Morven said.

"There are changing cubicles at the back of the enclosure," Annalies said.

All the soaked swimmers were making their way through the crowd that gathered around them to congratulate them on surviving the contretemps. Their shoulders were clapped and their hands were shaken. They were all bedraggled, their wet clothing clinging heavily to them.

Natasha thought it might be fun to be dunked into the water. It would certainly be a fast way to cool off!

The fourth oarsman came into view. He was making slow going of it, because so many people were stopping him to chat. His head was turned as he spoke. Just as the others did, the man's clothing clung to him. Natasha's heart gave a little squeeze, for this man wore no undershirt beneath his shirt. He had removed his jacket and rolled up his sleeves to row, just as all the rowers did and now the wet cotton molded itself against his chest. He had thick arms and powerful chest muscles. The clear silhouette narrowed down to a tight waist and hips. The soaked pants were wrapped around powerful thighs.

Something stirred, low in Natasha's belly. She held still, barely daring to breathe, as she realized she was responding to the sight of a man's body. She had never felt this stirring for any man but Seth. She remembered it well. The aching need had been absent for four years.

Now she was feeling it in response to the sight of a stranger.

She squeezed her legs together under her skirts, trying to deny her wantonness. She dismissed it, refusing to acknowledge the heavy tingling.

"Why, that's Raymond, isn't it?" Annalies asked.

Natasha's chest locked and her throat closed down, as the man she had been ogling turned his head back to continue on toward the cubicles.

It was Raymond. He had been laughing as he talked and the smile was still on his face. Ben must have convinced him to row, after all.

Then his eyes met hers and his smile faded.

Natasha didn't know what to do. She felt exposed by his gaze, as if he could see, as no one else could, the way her body was reacting to the sight of him. Her breath came faster. Her heart tottered at the impact of his gaze.

For a moment, the roar of the people around them fell away. It was as if only the two of them were there. In the silence, she could hear her heart and her frantic breath and nothing else.

Someone else thumped Raymond's shoulder, diverting his attention, tearing his gaze from her. At the same time, Morven Fortescue's elbow jostled Natasha, forcing her to clutch her stool to keep her balance.

"I am so terribly sorry," Morven said, grabbing her arm and helping her right herself. Then she swayed closer. "You were staring for far too long," she whispered.

Natasha looked at her, shocked, as she straightened her petticoats and dress.

Morven gave her a small smile. "I should like you to come to tea tomorrow. I will be at home. May I invite you?"

Shaken, Natasha could think of no suitably polite reason to refuse. She nodded, unable to speak.

Morven got to her feet. "I should return to Lady Gaddesby. I bid you good afternoon Princess Annalies, Lady Farleigh, Lady Innesford."

Annalies and Elisa made polite farewell comments, while Natasha could barely bring her thoughts together. She kept her head down, staring at the rows of pin tucks above the pleats of her dress, trying to recover quickly so no one else would suspect what had happened to her.

Her cheeks burned hot. She had been lusting for a man! And that man had been Raymond! How *could* she? It was so utterly inappropriate. It might even be sinful. How could she feel that way about the son of her best friend?

Sick fright was replacing the depraved ache she had been feeling. She was a wicked woman. A terrible one. How could she blight Seth's memory this way?

"She seems as though she is a very nice woman," Annalies observed.

"She is certainly very pretty. Her face is creamy, did you notice?"

"Pretty, yes, but not nearly as beautiful as Natasha," Annalies said stoutly, the loyal friend.

"They say the Scottish sun is kinder to ladies' faces. It seems it must be true. And she is very polite. Not one slip with our ranks, did you notice?"

Their chatter and their observations went on. They either had not noticed her distress, or had and were giving her time to recover. If they truly knew why she was distressed they would be appalled. Raymond was Elisa's son...oh, how could she possibly have felt anything at all?

Yet she had. Even before she had known who it was, Natasha had felt the yearning in her to be held, to be petted and stroked. A thousand such intimate moments with Seth had flashed through her mind, as she had hungrily skimmed her gaze over Raymond's body.

Seth had never let her get away with false coyness and she made herself face the truth now. She had lusted after a man. Yes, coincidentally, it had been a man she knew and that was unfortunate. Yet the whispering of women in private parlors, Annalies' own more shocking reviews of some of the books she liked to read, even Elisa and Vaughn's extended illicit collection of titles...they all admitted a woman could feel such urges. Some of them even argued that the urge to mate was a natural thing, and experiencing pleasure in the act was not just the province of whores.

Natasha drew in a deep breath, trying to relax. Her nausea eased and her heart slowed. She had felt a natural urge, she repeated to herself. No one had to know about it. She had no intention of acting upon it. It was the act that would make her sinful, not the impulse.

Elisa touched her wrist. "I'm told they will be serving ice cream in the luncheon tent. Shall we get some?"

"Oh, ice cream! I've never tasted anything so wonderful," Annalies said. "Yes, please, can we?"

Natasha let her two friends pull her onto her feet and link arms with her, glad they could not see into her mind, for they would recoil and draw away from her if they could.

* * * * *

Lilly hesitated at the door into the great library, for there were others already occupying the room. Will and Jack and Peter were all Elisa's sons, even though Will was the only natural born son and heir. Jack had been fostered by Elisa and Vaughn since he was a small child and Peter was adopted. All three of them, though, were mischief-makers supreme—even Peter, who at fifteen was four years younger than Will and Jack.

"I didn't know anyone was home," Lilly said awkwardly. She had rather counted on the library being deserted.

Jack sat up from his lounging in the button back club

chair and put his feet on the ground. "The racing at Hedley was halted early because someone had the lack of sense to sink a couple of boats." His heavy brows came together. "Damned inconvenient, if you ask me."

"Jack," Will said, his tone warning. He had propped himself against the reading table. He nodded his blond head toward Lilly.

"Sorry, Lilly."

"Was anyone hurt?" Lilly asked.

"Not a soul," Will said lightly. "Were you looking for a book for your lessons?"

"Actually I was looking for *Burke's Peerage.*"

All three of them paused to look at her, including Peter, perched high up on the ladder, his fine hair falling over his gray eyes.

"Why would you be wanting *Burke's*, Miss Lilly?" Jack crooned.

Her back stiffened. "Not for the reason you think," she said stiffly.

"Not hunting for a husband, then?"

She could feel her face heating. "Absolutely not."

"Why is that, anyway?" Peter asked. His voice was still high, only Lilly suspected that wouldn't last for long. His shoulders were filling out and his legs had always been long. He was going to be a tall man. "Doesn't every lady want a good marriage?"

Will looked up at him. "It's not that simple." He looked at Lilly. "Although he has a good question. Why *did* you agree to be governess for Mother?"

Her throat seemed to close over and squeeze. Lilly swallowed. "I will tell you why I want *Burke's*, if you agree not to tell anyone else," she said quickly, hoping it would deflect them.

"A secret?" Jack said.

Even Will looked interested.

Peter climbed down the ladder.

Lilly glanced over her shoulder. There was no one there. "I overheard Aunt Elisa and Mother and Aunt Anna talking in the garden one day. Do you remember, when it was very hot?"

All three of them nodded.

"They were talking about Raymond. I could hear it all through my bedroom window."

Jack rolled his eyes. "I thought you said it was a secret. You think we don't know everything about big brother Raymond?"

"Or made sure we found out?" Peter said, with a grin.

"Then you know he's been in secretly in love with a woman called Susanna for years and years?"

Silence.

Jack's gaze slid toward Will.

Will swiveled and pulled down the heavy volume from the shelf behind him. "*Burke's*. Last year's edition. If she's a peer, she'll be in there." He dumped it on the reading table.

Lilly closed the library door and moved over to stand behind Will and watch over his shoulder as he turned the pages.

So did Jack and Peter.

An hour later, they were staring defeat in the face. "Not a single Susanna," Jack said, disgusted, turning away.

"How many peers are there, anyway? Does *Burke's* have all of them?" Will asked.

"Most of them, I believe," Lilly said. "Aunt Annalies was right. Susanna isn't in it. She might be a commoner after all."

"That would explain why Raymond didn't marry her, wouldn't it?" Jack said, pouring two sherries from the decanter.

"*Sherry*, Jack?" Will said, astonished.

"It's past four," Jack pointed out. He handed Will the second glass. Will took it with a grin.

"Peers can marry commoners," Will said. "Look at Uncle Rhys."

"He's a very *uncommon* commoner," Jack said. He settled back in his club chair and put his legs over the arm. "Wasn't there a rumor at Cambridge? About Raymond and some mystery lady?"

Will crossed his arms. "Yes, I do recall that. I thought it was all a bit of nonsense made up because Raymond would never let himself been seen with *anyone*."

"Very private chap," Jack said in agreement. "Peter, give it up, lad. You won't find her in there."

Peter ran his finger down the page slowly, scanning each entry. "I just want to make sure," he said softly.

Lilly sighed. "Well, thank you," she told the boys.

"Remember, this stays between us, yes?"

"Absolutely," Will assured her.

"Certainly," Jack added, raising his glass toward her.

Lilly left them in the library and made her way back upstairs. She was uneasy about trying to pry loose Raymond's secret when, nearly a year ago, he had convinced her that to do so would be ruinous for the woman and perhaps for him, too. Surely, though, if Mother and Aunt Elisa and Aunt Anna were investigating, then it would be permissible for her to search, as well?

She just wanted to make sure Raymond wasn't driving himself into a deep and dark hole, as she had done. That was all. She was doing it for Raymond.

Chapter Four

Mulloy shook Natasha's shoulder. "I'm sorry to disturb you, my Lady. Lord Marblethorpe is in the drawing room, insisting upon seeing you."

"I'm not at home," Natasha said, keeping her head on the pillow. She was glad of the blankets and coverings that hid the way her heart jumped, and possibly hiding that her cheeks were turning pink, too. He was here!

"Corcoran told his lordship you were not at home, my lady, only he is still insisting. He said he would come up here and break down your door if you did not come downstairs. Corcoran thought it best I let you know rather than try to turn Lord Raymond away himself."

Natasha thought of elderly Corcoran trying to manhandle Raymond. She had a feeling Raymond would not put up with anyone trying to force him to do anything he did not want to do. It was wrong to leave Corcoran alone to deal with him.

Tiredly, she sat up.

Mulloy stepped back. "Shall I get you a wrapper, my lady?"

"Yes, I suppose so," Natasha said. She pushed the quilt aside and got to her feet. "Just linens, Mulloy. I shan't bother with a corset right now, as I intend to come straight back to bed once I've seen him off."

"Yes, my lady." Mulloy fluttered around Natasha, holding out a camisole and pantalets, then the wrapper. Natasha stretched and rubbed her eyes as Mulloy piled her hair up and pinned it in a fast, neat coil.

"Did you get *any* sleep, my lady?" Mulloy asked softly.

"Not really," Natasha admitted.

"That's three nights now. A body can't go on that long without *some* sleep."

"I agree," Natasha said with a sigh. "I would sleep if I could and sometimes I drift and *almost* fall asleep. Then I wake up, as if someone had snapped their fingers under my nose."

"It's a right puzzle, my lady. Why would you suddenly not be able to sleep like that? Do you think the air at Henley did something unnatural?"

Natasha carefully didn't meet Mulloy's eyes in the mirror. She felt guilty enough about the lies she was scattering about her. She knew exactly why she was not sleeping and it had nothing to do with the air at Henley.

As soon as Mulloy was finished, Natasha pushed herself to her feet, put on dance slippers and made her way downstairs. Corcoran met her at the foot of them. "Lord Marblethorpe is in the drawing room, my lady. Would you like me to accompany you?"

Natasha looked at him, startled. "Raymond is a family friend, Corcoran. Do you think I have need of a chaperone?"

Corcoran didn't unbend. "You don't seem quite yourself my lady, if you don't mind me saying so. You look in need of support and his lordship is not exactly…calm."

"I see," Natasha said. "I will call if I need assistance."

"Should I linger by the door, then, my lady?"

"That isn't necessary, Corcoran. If Raymond *is* upset, it is not with me. I have been in bed for three days, so the matter cannot involve me at all. Raymond is too much of a gentlemen to misdirect his anger. I will be quite safe."

Corcoran looked as though he wanted to argue. Natasha held his gaze until he nodded. "Very well, my lady." He walked stiffly away, his back straight.

Natasha pressed her hand against her churning innards and stepped into the drawing room.

Raymond was pacing at the other end of the room. When he saw her, he halted.

Natasha gripped the door handle and he held up his hand. "No, do not shut the door," he said quickly. "I would have no hint of impropriety leach from this room tonight."

She let the door handle go, as her heart lurched. Raymond really was here to speak to her about Henley. How mortifying! "If you have in mind to discuss what I suspect, then you should leave before you begin," she said stiffly. "This is not a conversation I intend to have."

He came up to her and her breath caught as he drew closer. He looked down at her. "You look as though you *should* speak of it," he said softly. "How long have you gone without sleep?"

His question confirmed that yes, Raymond had seen and recognized her reaction to him. It was doubly humiliating. Not only had she felt such inappropriate feelings, but he was aware of them, too.

There was nothing she could do. She had been utterly beggared before him. Her shame was complete.

Quite without realizing it, she raised her chin and looked at him directly. "Whatever the state of my health, it is of no concern to you, Lord Marblethorpe."

His mouth lifted a little. Warmth grew in his eyes. "You are courageous when the chips are down, aren't you? I knew that of course, only you remind me at every turn."

He was standing far too close to her for comfort. There was still a polite two feet between his boots and her hems, yet Natasha fancied she could feel the warmth of his body from where she stood.

She tore her attention away from his physicality. "You should not be speaking to me in this way."

"No, I shouldn't. Only, you should not have looked at me the way you did at Henley, either. It is as well you turned away when you did, lest someone other than me recognize the thoughts that prompted the look." He stepped back. "Come and sit down. Let Corcoran and the staff see you having a perfectly civilized conversation."

His caution, his sensitivity toward appearances, was reassuring. It let her move to the pair of Chesterfield chairs. She took the chair with its back to the door.

Raymond sat on the edge of the other, his knee almost brushing the edge of the chess table. He didn't speak, but studied her openly and for such a long time, she had to look away.

"Three nights of no sleep and still you outshine every

girl, woman and lady in London," he said softly.

"You should not be saying such things."

"I should not speak the truth?"

"Don't twist what I say."

"You do not appreciate a fine parry of words, then?"

"I prefer plain speaking." Seth had always cut directly to the core of anything.

"You always have," Raymond agreed. "All those society Romeos trying to breathe down one's bodice would have soured any woman. I imagine the rhetoric you have been forced to sift through has been legion."

"I am…I was a married woman. Men did not paw me."

"Not when Seth was alive, no. You really are lost without him, aren't you?"

Natasha met his gaze, startled. "Why are we talking about Seth? I thought you wished to speak of…" She pressed her lips together. Why was she forcing the conversation back to Henley? It was the last thing she wanted to discuss.

"We speak of Seth because he is the reason you've laid in your bed for three days, writhing with guilt over a perfectly natural function of womanhood."

Natasha pulled her wrapper closer about her. "It was an unfortunate moment. It won't happen again."

He didn't respond. His dark eyes gaze remained steady, as if he was casting about for an answer. Or observing her in disbelief.

Natasha shifted on the chair. "You insisted upon speaking about this, Raymond. Because of my behavior I am forced to endure the conversation. I would ask you to hurry up and complete it so I can return to my bed."

"This is the first time you've experienced any sort of arousal with a man other than Seth," he said, his tone one of amazement. He spoke softly, as if he was conversing with himself.

Natasha closed her eyes. She had thought she had reached the utter depths of her humiliation a few moments ago. Now she knew she was wrong.

"Natasha, look at me."

She could not sit there with her eyes closed forever. Sooner or later, she would have to look at him. She ground her teeth together, drew in a breath and opened her eyes.

He was not smiling. He was not leering at her for her lack of modesty, either. He was just sitting there.

"You are dear friends with Aunt Annalies," he said. "You should ask her to explain to you her theory on female sexuality. You might find it reassuring."

Natasha winced. "Is *nothing* beyond the bounds of polite conversation to you?"

"Oh, this is far beyond polite conversation," Raymond assured her. "We are family, remember? We can do as we please so long as no outsiders are made aware of our private activities. If you were a maiden at a ball, my conversation would be so chaste your mother would beam approval. You are not a maiden, though, and I have never been interested in whispering sweet nothings in a debutante's shell-like ear. Innocence may be virtuous, yet it is also utterly vapid."

"You and every man with red blood feels that way, I

wager," Natasha said. Her mouth fell open in surprise. Why had she said that?

Raymond merely smiled appreciation. "There. I knew you would fire back sooner or later."

"You want me to challenge you?" she asked, bewildered.

"I want you to be yourself," he said swiftly. "Not repressed by artificial morals that make you miserable and sick with guilt."

"Then...you do not think less of me?"

"How could I? My eyes were opened by that moment, too."

"They were?" She examined his face, to see if he was lying. His expression did not shift or his eyes cut away from her.

Then she realized what he was implying. "You mean you...too?"

He was sitting quite still and did not move at her question, yet it seemed to her he did grow more alert. More... tense. Her heart had been slowing and calming. Now it raced again.

"You say you prefer frankness. Let us speak frankly then and dispense with this conversation you find so uncomfortable," he said, his voice low.

Natasha wasn't sure she wanted plain truth now. Although she had stated she did and usually, yes, she preferred unadorned truth to the veiled misdirection and coy vagueness that peppered most polite conversations. She nodded. Laying out unvarnished fact would at least end this quickly.

Raymond leaned forward and dropped his voice so there

was absolutely no chance of anyone standing by the door hearing him. "I am sure you tire of people telling you how beautiful you are, yet you have not fully absorbed what that means. A dozen pretty faces can be found at any soiree. Yours is a greater beauty than that. Time does not touch it and every man is moved by it…and not just to spout odes in acknowledgement. Yours is the beauty that drives men to drink, to duel over your favors and to dream of what it may be like to have you not just in their arms, but in their bed."

Natasha swallowed. "Raymond…"

"I am a man," Raymond said. "Yes, your beauty stirs me, too. More than that, when I realized at Henley you were not indifferent to me…" He let out a heavy breath. "You are not alone in losing sleep, Natasha."

Her heart actually stopped. For a moment, she felt weightless, as she might in a dream. The flesh between her thighs throbbed.

His words formed an image in her mind, of a big man's heated body against hers. It wasn't an image from a gentle romance, where a chaste kiss on the wrist was the epitome of love. No, it was an earthy, raw image. The man was naked and she could feel his excitement held against her and she welcomed it and wanted more.

That big man was Raymond.

Natasha let out a breath that shook. "You…" She cleared her throat. "You would propose we indulge in these animal instincts, then?"

"No."

Disappointment touched her. Then confusion. How

could she be disappointed?

Raymond's gaze was drilling into hers, not letting her go. He could likely see her every thought, just as he seemed to have plucked all her thoughts and feelings from her at Henley. "I propose that for now, you simply acknowledge that you have them. You champion the truth, you say. Then be truthful to yourself. Or tell me you felt nothing at Henley and I will leave right now and never speak more than polite nothings to you ever again."

It would be so simple to say she felt nothing. It would remove him from her house and her life. Only...

Even these few moments of sharing private thoughts with a man had brought back to her the warmth and intimacy of her time with Seth. She had thought she missed Seth. Now she realized how much more she had lost. They had been closest friends as well as lovers and spouses. Natasha had hidden nothing of herself from him. Seth had known her every petty thought, her dreams and wishes, hopes and fantasies and had accepted them completely and unconditionally. Even her flaws and human weaknesses had merely been what he called the leavening in her soul. She missed that complete acceptance. She missed conversations where she did not have to mind her tongue or apologize for her thoughts.

And she missed being held.

She sheared away from that whispering yearning.

"Natasha?" Raymond prompted her.

Natasha looked at him. "Frankness, you said?"

"Yes," he said flatly.

"I would acknowledge Henley," she said, "except that I am afraid of where it will lead us. I do not know what is in your thoughts, Raymond, but there can never been anything between us. You know that, don't you? Society would crucify us. Your mother would...would at the very least destroy our friendship and that I count as a higher cost."

"Are you sure those things would happen?" Raymond asked softly. There was a challenging note in his voice.

She skirted the question. "If I say yes, what do you intend to do?"

"Nothing that you do not want me to do."

It was not a reassuring answer.

"If you say no, Natasha, even if you lie to say it, then I will understand," he said quietly. "It is completely your decision." His black eyes glowed with a held-back heat. "What do you want?"

She twined her fingers and squeezed hard. "I want..." She cleared her throat again. *Truth*, she reminded herself. It had been so long since she had been free to speak unadorned truth!

"I want us to be friends," she said slowly. "I have not had a friend...not a...a male friend, since Seth died and I miss that companionship terribly. Only..."

"Nothing more?" he finished.

She shook her head, frustrated. "Oh, this is so very awkward. I am conflicted, Raymond." She touched her fingers to her chest. "I would speak the truth if I did not fear the complications that come with it. The sort of friendship I would prefer would let me speak that truth without fear. Yet it would not compromise my position, either." She dropped her hand. "I do not think such a friend could exist. It would be asking too much of any man. It would not be fair."

Raymond's gaze wouldn't let her go. "Ask it of me."

Her heart actually hurt, it beat so hard. It seemed to leap in her chest. "Would you...could you be that sort of friend, Raymond?" Her lips seemed thick and uncooperative.

"I will be whatever friend you want me to be and consider it the greatest of privileges." Still he did not move. The tension that held him seemed to increase.

"Then yes," Natasha told him. "I was moved by the sight of you, at Henley."

He let out a gusty sigh and sat back, relaxing all at once. "And...?" he prompted, his brow lifting.

"...and I have not slept since," she added. "For fear you would think me a whore for enjoying such a sight and take advantage of it."

"Yet here I sit, clearly not disgusted or lecherous."

"Not even by my brazen language," she added. She could feel her mouth trying to tug into a smile.

"There is a freedom in being able to call a whore a whore and a spade a spade," he confessed.

The impulse to smile, or even laugh faded. "No one can know about this, Raymond," she added. "Even within the family, they would be shocked. Your mother..." She hesitated, fear blooming.

"I think you underestimate my mother. However, this is your friendship, to shape as you see fit." He got to his feet. "It is pleasing to me that you feel comfortable enough to show me your real self."

"You're leaving?" she asked, startled.

"Yes."

"But…" She bit her lip, confused.

He stopped by her chair and looked down at her. "Did you think that once I had secured your confession, I would press myself upon you? Force you to extend the boundaries of the friendship by seduction?"

"Yes," she said flatly. "That is what men do," she added.

He glanced toward the door, checking for observers, then crouched down next to the chair. It put his head level with hers. This close, she could see the thickness of his black lashes and the scar on his chin. She could even detect his scent, mixed up with the heat of his body, which washed over her like a wave. He smelled different from the way she remembered Seth's scent. That was to be expected, yet it was also reassuring. She didn't want him to be the same in any way.

She wondered if he would kiss her and how she could stop him if he tried.

"You think I want to kiss you, yes?" he said softly.

She nodded.

"I do, only not badly enough to ruin your good opinion of me." Instead, he reached over and very gently brushed a strand of loose hair from her forehead. His fingers barely grazed her flesh, yet she shivered at the touch. "You are too muddied by exhaustion to be thinking very clearly at all. When you have rested, we can talk more, if you wish. I suspect you will sleep very well, now."

She thought so, too. She could already feel the bone-deep weariness settling in. "When will I see you again?"

"Whenever you want." He got to his feet. His smile was small and warm. "It is nine in the morning, but I would wish you a good night."

She smiled. "Good night, Raymond."

Natasha listened to him move out into the front hall, intending to get up and return upstairs herself. It was the last thought she had until Mulloy woke her some indeterminate time later and helped her walk sleepily upstairs.

She didn't wake again until the next morning.

Chapter Five

The day after the Henley incident, Morven, Lady Tachbrook, had sent Natasha an invitation to visit her at home. Natasha had promptly declined.

The day after sleeping almost around the clock, though, another beautifully scribed missive sat among Natasha's morning letters. Morven would be at home again, this afternoon.

Natasha frowned at the page as she ate a generous breakfast, trying to decide how to deal with the insistent woman. A second invitation after a first refusal was perfectly acceptable. If Natasha turned down this second invitation, though, it would be sending a clear signal that she did not want to associate with Morven on a social level. Yet, Natasha had allowed the woman to write to her. If she refused a second time, it would make her dishonest.

True, she had agreed to Morven contacting her while under the strain of other matters…

Natasha realized what she was doing, even in her own thoughts and corrected it, her cheeks warming, just while sitting alone at the table. When Morven had asked if she could write, Natasha had been fuzzy and bemused by the sight of Raymond's damp and nearly nude body. It was the truth, only it was not an excuse she could use to get out of this, therefore she must suffer through at least one social engagement with Morven Fortescue, before declining any more invitations.

Morven was living in a hotel on Duke Street, not far from where Rhys had once lived as a bachelor. The establishment was high-class, with a flawless reputation. As a temporary accommodation, it would not sully a widow's reputation to be seen there, although she did wonder why Morven would not stay with friends, if she did not have a townhouse of her own in London.

Morven answered the question when they settled into the private loungeroom, even though Natasha had not asked directly. "My accommodations must seem odd to you, as you have such an extended family and friends. I told you I had lived an isolated life in Scotland for many years. Friendships withered as a result and I have no family to call upon. Neither did my husband. The title died with him." She smiled softly. "I considered purchasing a townhouse, only I am so rarely in London that the expense does not justify itself." She rested her hand against the teapot, checking the heat.

"Then you are returning to Scotland soon?" Natasha asked politely.

"I never intended to stay for the Season," Morven confessed. "Such frivolities are not for me."

"Your charity work is your only interest?"

"For a very long time, I did not have even that," Morven said, pouring two cups of tea. She handed one to Natasha. "It can be unbearable when one's husband dies. It took a great deal of time for my interest in life to return. Your awakening was much faster than mine." She smiled.

Natasha's innards jumped. "I have no idea what you mean," she said stiffly.

Morven sipped. "I do not believe anyone else noticed how closely you watched Lord Marblethorpe at Henley. I deflected your interest quickly enough the gossips may not have had time to turn away from the delectable sight of men in wet clothing." She smiled and her smile was full of mischief. "I rather think the experience of lusting after a man is new to you, since your husband passed. Yes?"

Natasha stared at her. She could think of nothing to say. Shock and horror curled through her. She realized she was holding her teacup in midair and put it back on the saucer with an unsteady hand. "I...er..."

"Will you be pursuing your interest, Lady Innesford? I ask not from a prurient view point, but because I would be happy to help, if that is your intent."

Natasha's horror grew. "No!" she said, her voice strangled and weak. "I could not possibly... *Pursue?*" she repeated, the implications behind the word impacted all over again. "You make it sound as if...as if..." She shook her head.

Morven put her cup down. She was smiling. "Oh dear," she said, sounding not at all distressed. "You are rather innocent, despite marriage and...how many children have you?"

"Seven," Natasha said automatically, staring at the woman. Her mind was exploding with all sorts of strange ideas and realizations. "Have you...extended your help to other...

women?"

"Ladies, all of them," Morven said gently. "Not many, no. There are few who are honest enough about their thoughts and feelings to encompass more sophisticated forms of pleasure."

"Is that what they are?" Natasha said distantly. She felt as though she had been tipped into Alice's rabbit hole.

"Certainly," Morven said firmly. "Pleasures of the flesh, although the Queen would have women think lifting their eyes above the drudgery of child birth and home-keeping a mortal sin."

Natasha looked at her with growing horror. "Is this the secret of your charm? Is this how you manage to raise so much money? By arranging…."

Morven actually laughed. "Good lord, no," she said, when she had herself under control. "Charm and education are my weapons when it comes to that. These pleasures I speak of are a very private aspect. I know you understand that sort of discretion. Your Great Family…well, it is really the three families that cling together so tightly, isn't it? Others say it is nearly impossible to be included in the inner circle of your family and friends. The strength of the bonds that bind you together are widely envied, only I suspect those bonds include an iron boundary of discretion, too. You protect each other."

Natasha deliberately drew in a slow, controlled breath, deep into her lungs, as far as her corset would let her. Then she let it out and felt a little control return to her. "You have a rather exalted view of my friends," she said gently. "We have known each other for a very long time, that is all. There is no iron boundary, as you say."

Morven nodded. "Of course, you would say that. I am aware, though, of the scandals that have dogged all of you in the past. That would bring you together, wouldn't it? It would make you want to work together to shield yourselves from further notoriety."

Natasha give her a stiff smile and sipped her tea to give herself time to think. "I don't know you nearly well enough to begin to respond," she said.

"That is a very sensible attitude," Morven said approvingly. "You really do not know me at all and therefore have no reason to trust me. I would feel exactly the same way if I were you. I did want to extend my offer of help, despite the risk of shocking you. You are a widow, too. I know what your life must be like." She sipped her tea while Natasha scrambled to find a way to respond.

Morven spoke again before Natasha could. "Of course, Lord Marblethorpe is part of the family, isn't he? Lady Farleigh's oldest son…he would be well inside the iron boundary that you say does not exist." She spoke softly, as if she was thinking to herself.

Natasha felt the heat swoop up from her belly, flushing her face and neck and making the hair on the back of her neck prickle. She was helpless to stop it and aware that it was an unmistakable signal that Morven would not fail to see.

Morven's generous mouth curved up into a smile and her blue eyes twinkled. "I thought so," she said complacently. She patted the back of Natasha's hand where it rested on the table. "I would wish you luck, only I saw the look on his Lordship's face, too. I don't believe you will need to do more than hold your breath and let him trip you." She straightened up and picked up the teapot. "Are you attending Lady Shelburne's Sweet Pea Ball next week?"

The invitation to the ball was still sitting on the desk in the library. "I haven't attended the ball for years," Natasha said bluntly, still too uncomfortable to bother with pretty phrases and prevarications.

"Since your husband passed?" Morven guessed. "Perhaps you should consider attending this year. Dancing is one of the best ways to drive a man to desperation…but then, I'm sure you knew that already." Her gaze met Natasha's.

"I determined that for myself when I was seventeen," Natasha replied. She felt her mouth open and her eyes widen.

Morven gave another merry laugh. "I almost feel sorry for Marblethorpe!"

✳ ✳ ✳ ✳ ✳

Natasha stepped out of the carriage almost before it had stopped, yanked her hoops back into place impatiently and hurried up the three short steps and used the door knock with energy.

The door was opened almost immediately—by Raymond.

"I saw you through my window," he said and glanced over her shoulder and up and down the street.

Natasha stepped back, doubt tearing at her suddenly. "Is this wrong? Should I not have come here?"

Raymond made an impatient sound. "You should do exactly what you want to do. I look, only to see who might observe I'm not wearing my jacket. If you don't mind that, come in. Otherwise, I must shut the door and dress properly, then open it again."

"I've seen you in less," Natasha said.

Raymond laughed and stood aside. "You'd better come in then."

She slipped inside and Raymond shut the door. "I have this, thank you, Thomsett," he told his butler, who was only just hurrying through from the back rooms.

Thomsett halted and nodded. "Tea, sir?"

"I won't stay long," Natasha said, already feeling uncomfortable about the impulse that had driven her here.

"No, thank you, Thomsett," Raymond told him. He waved toward a front room. The morning room, Natasha guessed. She had never been here before, although everyone knew where the Devlin family townhouse was located. She went through and was pleasantly surprised by the airiness of the room, the pretty roses and the arrangement of the furniture. She didn't sit down, though. Her discomfort was increasing.

Raymond pushed his hands into his trouser pockets. "You are almost vibrating. What has happened to bring you pounding on my door?"

Natasha tore off her gloves. Her hands were sweaty. "I have just come from Duke Street. I had tea with a woman who said things…" She took a breath. "Perhaps I should leave. It was silly to think that I…" She bit her lip.

"That you…?" Raymond asked.

"It's just that I could speak to Seth about anything!" she said in a rush. "I could ask questions and not feel like a fool."

"Ask me, if that is what you want," Raymond said.

Natasha calmed herself. She smoothed her hands down her gabardine skirt. "Is it true that there is a…a layer of people who…do what they please, when they please, with whomever they please? That they help each other do it?"

"Ah…" Raymond lifted a brow. "Who was it who opened your eyes, then?"

"Morven, Lady Tachbrook."

"I don't know the lady or the name," Raymond confessed.

"A Scots baronet. She was standing next to me at Henley."

Raymond's smile was warm. "I failed to notice anyone but you at Henley."

Her heart gave a little trip hammer and hurried on. "Is it true, then? There are people out there who freely…"

"Freely indulge in sexual partners? Oh yes," he said softly. "There have been people like that throughout history. However, they are usually more discreet than to blurt it out over tea and crumpets."

"She told me because…" Natasha halted, aware of what

she would have to say to finish the sentence, and who she was saying it to.

Raymond raised his brows. "Something about me, perhaps?" he guessed.

"Yes!" Natasha said, relief touching her. "She wanted to help me. She said she would help me…trip you."

Raymond laughed. It was a deep belly laugh, filled with humor.

Natasha could feel her own lips twitch. "I suppose, if I really had wanted to trip you, I just showed you my hand, didn't I?"

"Indeed," he replied, sobering. "Although you would have no need of card tricks to achieve that, if you wanted it. You have but to ask."

Natasha's breath whooshed out of her. She scrambled to remember what she had wanted to say.

Raymond smiled. "I like disconcerting you."

"I'm afraid mention of…of…*sex*," she added firmly, "will *always* disconcert me."

"You said you could say anything to Seth," he reminded her. "Just not sex?"

"I didn't have to speak of sex, when I merely had to reach out…" She drew in a breath. "You are distracting me," she said firmly, gathering her thoughts together. "Raymond, are there really people who have sex simply for the sake of having sex?"

"Yes."

"Morven made it sound affectionless and calculated. I cannot imagine how it could be pleasurable if the affection is not there."

"Sex without love, is what you mean. Sex without love is a poor substitute. It is better than nothing, though," Raymond said softly.

"Than not having sex at all? How could it be?"

"The act itself generates a weak substitute for love. It engenders intimacy." He shrugged. "There is a reason prostitutes exist, beyond merely giving men a vent for natural urges."

Natasha stared at him. "Did you...I mean have you...?"

Raymond's gaze was steady. "Have you ever indulged yourself, Natasha?"

"With another person? Never," she said firmly.

"I mean, by yourself. Because it was pleasurable."

Natasha couldn't look at him. Her face was burning again. She couldn't even form an answer. She *wouldn't* answer.

"Those who find pleasure with other people are doing as you do by yourself, only with the other person there, it creates a small amount of intimacy and companionship that is usually missing in their lives."

Natasha cleared her throat. She still couldn't look at him.

"And yes, there are some people who do it simply because they like the act itself and cannot have enough of it—sometimes more than a single partner can provide."

Natasha glanced down at her hands, where she was smoothing her skirt in constant motion. She made her hands stop. "I feel as ignorant as I did when I was seventeen and discovered I had a half-brother who everyone had lied to me about for my entire life."

Raymond lifted her chin, making her look at him. His fingers were firm. "You are unaware of such things because you have always been loved and sheltered, that is all. The people this Morven talks about are often troubled, their hearts broken by transitory affairs, diseases, pregnancies and more. It seems bohemian to recklessly embrace free love, yet it comes with a price. Such matters are hidden away from gentle souls like you, because they are unpleasant."

"Only, they are true, aren't they?" she replied. "It is like when Annalies first told Elisa and I about the homeless, wretched children living in squalor right here in London. We didn't believe her until she showed us. Only then could we do something to help them. If we had remained ignorant about that unpleasantness, then Elisa and Anna would never have adopted their children and I would not have thought to help establish the Orphans Society. Shielding people from harsh truths doesn't work, Raymond."

"Shielding *you* may not work," he replied, his tone one of agreement. "There are many people who are perfectly happy to move through life in complete ignorance of harsh realities."

"My mother was one of them," Natasha admitted. She met his gaze. It was far easier now to do that. "Please do not shield me anymore, Raymond. I would prefer to know whatever it is I do not know."

"Such as how badly I want to kiss you right now?" he asked.

Her body seemed to tingle. Her breath stopped. Then

she shook her head. "You did it again."

"Disconcerted you. Yes." His smile was warm.

"Do you? Want to kiss me, I mean?"

"You asked for the truth, remember?"

Her breasts seemed to swell inside her corset. She grew aware of the tips, brushing gently against the cotton of her camisole. Her heart raced.

Yet Raymond made no move toward her. He stayed utterly still, except for his hand in his pockets. They were curled into hard fists, she realized.

"I should go," she said slowly, staring at the tight balls of his fists, lifting the fabric of his trousers. "It would not be nice to linger here and dangle something I am not prepared to give. Besides, I promised Anna and Elisa I would stop by after tea with that woman."

"To report on her?" Raymond asked.

"They thought she was such a nice woman," Natasha admitted. "All the way here from Duke Street I was thinking just the opposite. Now, I just feel sorry for her. Her life is truly empty of friends and family and she uses sex to fill the void."

"How very astute of you," Raymond said softly. "Will you tell Anna and my mother that?"

Natasha smiled. "If I can find a way to tell them that doesn't mention you, I will. Neither of them prefer ignorance, either."

* * * * *

The three of them sat in Elisa's boudoir, on the edges of their chairs so they could lean closer and keep their voices down as they discussed every aspect of Natasha's visit with Morven Fortescue. Natasha had let them think Morven was the one who lusted after one of the other rowers, which left Raymond out of the discussion entirely.

"I still cannot believe she would ask you to help her seduce the man, though," Elisa said. It was not the first time she had said it. "It is rather cheeky."

"I imagine she thought Natasha would be practiced at it," Anna said. "Men make fools of themselves around her all the time."

"I am practiced at not letting them trap me in corners," Natasha said shortly. "Encouraging them is an entirely different matter."

"Does any man have to be encouraged?" Elisa asked. "It seems to me they tend to make up their own minds."

"If they believe the woman is available, then yes," Anna said. "Otherwise, wouldn't it simply be a matter of letting them know one is secretly available?"

Natasha gave a little shudder. "It is all so very clandestine and underhanded. Marriage is much easier."

"If one loves their husband, then yes," Anna said. "We three are very lucky in that regard."

Elisa shook her head. "We risked scandal and complete ruin, all of us, to marry the man we loved. It's not the same thing at all. Anna, imagine if you had been married off to a suitable Duke or Prince. Do you imagine you would feel the same way about marriage and the bedroom, then?"

Anna took off her spectacles and rubbed the bridge of her nose. "I would think not," she said quietly. "I remember as a child and a new woman thinking that marriage would be an escape from the torments at home, only now I have Rhys," and she smiled, her eyes suddenly glowing, "I can see how such a marriage would be just another torment."

"My mother forced an engagement with a man called Sholto Piggott upon me," Natasha said and shuddered.

"I was going to marry Vaughn's father," Elisa added. "I cannot even imagine what the marriage bed would have been like, had I not met Vaughn."

Silence fell between them as they contemplated what might have been.

Then Elisa stirred. "Besides, I didn't ask you here to talk about that poor woman." She glanced over her shoulder once more, even though the door to the suite had been firmly shut for a good hour. Then she leaned forward again. "I spoke to Raymond about Susanna."

Natasha caught her breath. So did Annalies, yet there was a gleam of interest in her eyes that Natasha did not share.

"What did he say?" Annalies asked.

"Well, he did not deny the woman existed," Elisa admitted. "He would tell me nothing of her. He said almost exactly what he told Natasha, that it would damage too many reputations to explain more."

Annalies nodded. "Did he give any hints at all?"

Natasha gripped her hands together, wondering how she might contrive to look as interested as Annalies in the identity of the mystery woman, yet in truth, she did not.

A month ago, she would have had no hesitation talking about Raymond at all. The lives of their children were constantly filleted and analyzed by the three of them. Many of the major decisions in the rearing of their children had been made in such a circle of conversation.

Yet now, it felt wrong to be sitting here discussing Raymond and she wanted to writhe in her discomfort.

"No hints at all," Elisa said. "He assured me there was absolutely no hope of uniting with her, though."

"Really?" Annalies breathed. "It's all rather tragic, isn't it?"

Elisa nodded. "I advised him to move on with his life and try to put the woman behind her. He said he was, indeed, taking action to do just that."

Annalies looked disappointed. "We may never know who Susanna is, then."

"Perhaps it is just as well. The less we prod the matter, the quicker Raymond can move on."

Natasha stared down at her hands, folded neatly in her lap. Raymond was getting on with his life, leaving his old love behind. Wasn't that exactly what she had been doing these last few weeks? In that, they were alike, Raymond and her. It gave them even more in common.

No wonder she had been drawn to him. There was an underlying foundation they shared.

That made the friendship between them genuine, not just an invention of her lonely imagination. The realization relieved her.

"Has he really been in love with her for years?" Annalies asked. "What else did he say?"

Natasha rose to her feet abruptly. "I am sorry," she told them both, as they looked up at her, surprised. "I have lingered here far longer than I should have. I promised the twins and Lisa Grace I would play quoits with them before supper and it is getting quite late."

"You do indulge your children," Elisa observed, as she did whenever Natasha spoke of keeping company with the children outside the usual post supper visit.

"They have demonstrated no harm from the practice," Annalies said. "In some ways, Elisa, they are highly affectionate and well-grounded people. At least, the adults appear to be…so far." She smiled at Natasha. "There is plenty of time for the children to involve themselves in a scandal, yet."

Natasha smiled, even though she was uncomfortable with the lie she had just spoken. "Scandal is a family tradition, after all," she finished.

As she settled into the carriage, Natasha reflected that it was entirely possible she herself was creating a brand new scandal of her own.

* * * * *

After Natasha had left, Elisa glanced at Annalies, where they stood in the front hall where they had bid Natasha goodbye.

"That was rather odd," Elisa said.

"You do rattle on at her about her lax ways with the

children," Anna pointed out.

"That was after 'tasha said she was leaving," Elisa said, frowning. "Did we say something to upset her?"

"We were talking about Raymond before that."

"Mmm," Elisa said.

"I have time for one more cup of tea before I leave," Anna said. "It will give me just enough time to tell you about the letter I got from Eton yesterday, about Iefan."

"Has he been suspended again?" Elisa asked.

Anna laughed. "He argued with his science master that light is an electromagnetic wave and part of the electromagnetic spectrum, not a separate entity in its own right."

"He disputed his teacher?" Elisa said, shocked. The two of them moved toward the drawing room.

"Yes, and produced the papers published by Professor Maxwell three years ago to substantiate the claim. Really, I cannot see what the fuss is about. Iefan was perfectly correct."

Elisa shook her head. "You approve of what he did!"

"Oh, he should not have called his science master a buffoon, I grant you," Anna said dismissively.

Elisa laughed. "You are irrepressible, Princess Annalies."

"Only in the company of my closest friends, of course," Annalies said with a smile. Her smile faded as they settled about the card table. "I do hope Natasha is not upset with us. She didn't speak at all when we were talking about Raymond."

"Natasha doesn't always have an opinion about everything the way you do," Elisa replied.

Annalies looked surprised. "I do not!" Then she frowned. "Besides, everyone has an opinion about everything, simply because they are capable of reasoning. She must have had an opinion of some sort."

Elisa smiled.

"What did I say?"

"You just proved my point, my dear."

Annalies looked startled. Then they both laughed.

Chapter Six

It was a relief to realize she was awake, after all.

Natasha lay on her back, the bedlinens tangled around her hips and legs, her heart thudding and her skin damp with exertion. The room was silent and almost completely dark, except for a strip of moonlight creeping in through the curtains.

The dream had been extremely vivid—far more than usual. Even now, though, the details were slipping away. She was left with an impression of hands on her body and the weight of another against her, as every inch of her was stroked and teased, her nerves brought to life with crackling intensity.

As she lay recovering, Natasha moaned. Her real body, not just her dream body, was throbbing with the power of those hands. The tips of her breasts were hard and the delicate motion of her nightdress across them felt like the teasing touch of a lover.

The flesh between her legs throbbed.

This heated state of her body was how Seth had often made her feel. She hadn't experienced such an intense longing since he had gone…except for a pale echo when she had watched Raymond at Henley. This need she felt now was as powerful as any Seth had ever stirred in her. She moved restlessly, pushing the bedclothes off with her feet.

It still wasn't enough. She rose and went to the window and pulled the curtains aside. The moonlight fell through the lace sheers, to pattern her body with shadowy flourishes and flowers.

She reached past the lace and lifted the window up, opening it wide.

Immediately, night sounds came to her. It was very late. The gas lanterns had been extinguished and Hyde Park was swathed in shadows. Because there was no traffic on the street, she could hear the wind in the tree tops across Park Lane. She could smell the early morning coolness of the air, redolent with green, growing things and moisture.

Natasha breathed deeply, inhaling it all.

Raymond was also lying in a bed, only a few blocks from here. He would be sleeping, as was most of London was at this time. She preferred to think he was not. Was he thinking of her again? Was he wondering what it would be like to kiss her?

How things had changed in the last few weeks! Raymond had gone from being Elisa's grown son in her mind, to a man who could make her feel this way just by looking at her.

Natasha went back to the bed and gathered the nightdress up in her hand so she could climb onto the mattress. Her knee was almost as pale as the sheet in the ghostly moonlight.

She settled on the bed on her knees, her hand still clenching the nightdress, watching the lace at the window billow softly. Then, with a compulsive jerk, she pulled the dress off and dropped it onto the end of the bed where the bedclothes were bundled.

The air breezing through the window played over her naked body and she drew in a shaky breath as the fever in her blood boiled. Her breasts were aching to be touched, the tips almost hurting.

She put her hands over them and shuddered at the brush of her palms against the nipples. If her own touch could do this, what would another's hands feel like? What would a mouth feel like?

Natasha moaned, as fragments of her dream came back to her and dropped her hand to the junction of her thighs and pressed the fingers against her mound. She watched the wind move the curtain at the window as she spread her knees and curved her fingers deeper between her thighs.

The wetness there was not a surprise to her. The heat was. It was as if she was burning.

The touch of her fingers against the inner flesh made her eyes drift shut. She pushed the tips up against the nub and felt the swollen sensitivity of it. Her hips thrust forward at the touch and her climax gathered almost instantly, building rapidly.

She let her head fall back, feeling the brush of her hair against her rear and stroked quickly. The pleasure peak was so close and needed little encouragement.

Natasha came with a groan. She held it in, her jaw clamped, as her body shuddered and the pleasure sizzled through her. The intensity of the sensations was almost frightening.

Slowly, her breath ease, her heart calmed and sense returned. She looked at the open window and the moving curtain and shivered. She reached for the nightgown and put it on, feeling the chill of the air. Moving quickly, she straightened out the blankets and sheets and slid beneath them.

Her gaze fell on the untouched pillow on the other side of the bed. Natasha put her hand on the pillow. "Please understand," she whispered.

With her hand on the pillow, she closed her eyes and wished for a dreamless sleep.

* * * * *

William Wardell was a handsome man. He was the same age as Lilly, which made him a little too young for Lilly's tastes. She had never considered Will as anything more than an unofficial cousin and a good friend, although he had a wicked sense of fun and they had had their share of scrapes over the years.

It had been several years, though, since he had beckoned her into the carriage to plot more mischief and Lilly stepped out of the town house and into the brougham with a sense of trepidation. She could not afford to be entangled in one of Will's grand messes. Not anymore.

Will shifted over to the edge of the seat as she stepped inside the carriage. He was dressed for walking, which told her he was heading for Hyde Park. He had been growing a pointed, trimmed beard for about a year, now, although the unruly mop of thick sandy hair was still not restrained. His habit of running his hand through his hair did not help with the lack of neatness. His smile was warm.

Lilly settled on the seat next to him, arranged her hems and took off her spectacles. "I cannot stay long," she warned him. "Some of us have to work, you know."

"God, I'd hate to have you as a governess," Will said. "Teaching Latin conjugates has soured you. You've lost all your humor since you took the post."

"Your mother doesn't want the girls to learn Latin just yet. I focus on deportment and history, literature and mathematics."

"As I said," Will replied. He lifted up a heavy book from where it had been tucked between him and the carriage wall and held it out. "Peter found something."

Lilly put her glasses back on as Will opened *Burke's* to a page that had been marked with a strip of torn stationery. He placed the book on her lap and pointed.

Lilly read the entry. "Linnea Susan Donaldson?" she repeated aloud.

"*Susan*," Will repeated for emphasis. He tapped the page. "She has not married, to date."

Lilly peered at the birthdate. "She is nearly thirty. I would guess that marriage is not in her future, either."

"Exactly," Will said.

"She isn't Susanna, though."

"Peter thought that maybe Susanna was a family name."

"A family name?"

"You're Lillian, only we all call you Lilly. Everyone calls me Will. Your father was Richard, yet everyone used his middle name, Seth." Will shrugged. "A family name."

Lilly pursed her lips. "It is a bit thin, isn't it?"

"She's the only Susan in the book who fits," Will said. "Look at her ancestry. The Donaldsons are from Hertfordshire."

Lilly shook her head, lost.

"Farleigh Hall is in Hertfordshire." Will pointed to the entry. "Raymond grew up near her. She's close to his age. And she is still unmarried. Her middle name is Susan, which could easily become Susanna." He shrugged.

"It's a little more convincing," Lilly admitted. "But hardly conclusive."

"You sound more like a governess every day," Will said. "*Conclusive.*"

Lilly let the petty hurt roll over her and depart. Then she said, "What are you proposing? Do you intend to write to the lady and demand she admit she threw Raymond over?"

"The first half is already done," Will said. He frowned. "That is where we are mired." He pulled an envelope out of his jacket. It was crumpled and the seal broken. "The letter was returned this morning. Her family's secretary said she was living in Paris. He gave me the address and suggested I redirect the letter there."

"The family read the letter?" Lilly asked, surprised and more than a little uncomfortable.

Will shook his head. "They returned it unopened. They might have sent it on," he added, mildly irritated.

"Couriers to Paris are expensive," Lilly said.

"Not if they're already going there." Will put the letter

back in his jacket. "Jack and Peter and I are going to Paris to see her."

"No, Will, you can't simply turn up on her doorstep like that!" Lilly protested. "Even if the lady *is* Susanna, she would hardly break down and confess to a stranger who arrives unannounced! It's madness!"

"I do wish you'd give me some credit," Will said. "It's summer, Lilly. Everyone is travelling right now. Jack and I will take Peter to see Paris for the first time. What could be more natural? And while we're there, we will accidentally bump into an English lady who is from Hertfordshire, the same as our older cousin, what a coincidence, and all that…" He shrugged.

Lilly pressed her lips together. "You are not asking me to go with you, are you? Because I cannot, of course. I have the girls to take care of."

Will shook his head. "We thought we should let you know about this," and he tapped the book, "as this business all started with you."

"I do appreciate your thoughtfulness, Will. You will write to me and tell me how it goes?"

"Of course." He kissed her cheek. "Back off to work, Lady Governess," he told her and reached over her to open the carriage door.

"Enjoy Paris!" she told him and climbed down to the footpath.

"It is Paris," he called after her. "What is there *not* to enjoy?"

It was as if her mind and her body and her senses were all waking up after a very long hibernation. Before her nighttime study of the moonlight, Natasha had become aware of how her energy and enthusiasm for even simple, everyday things had increased. Eating had become enjoyable again. After that moon-filled night, though, every day seemed to be alive with possibilities. She was filled with vigor. It was hard to maintain a sedate stroll in the park each day, when what she really wanted to do was stride...or run.

She had even caught herself humming.

The idea of attending Lady's Shelburne's Sweet Pea Ball did not seem quite so dismaying as before. More enticing was the idea of dancing. She had not danced for years. Not since Seth had died. Not even a sedate Schottische. Even watching other dancers had not stirred her.

Now, though, Natasha wanted to dance. She accepted Lady Shelburne's invitation with an apology for the late response. With only a day or two to plan for the ball, Natasha was at a loss to know what to wear. She had no ball gowns anymore, although once, she had owned dozens.

Then she remembered the silver lace gown. It had been ordered the week before Seth died and never worn. It was possibly still in the box the Parisian designer had delivered it in. As the French had been wearing hoops well ahead of the English adopting them, the gown was still fashionable, four years later.

Vaughn and Elisa, Annalies and Rhys were all attending

the ball. Nearly the entire adult contingent of the family would be there, for the ball was one of the highlights of the Season. Even Anna and Rhys's oldest son, Iefan, was attending. He had just turned sixteen. Most of the girls in the family were younger, though, and not ready to be debutantes yet. With so many of the family there, Natasha did not have to worry about appearing unescorted.

When the evening arrived, Natasha vibrated with impatience for the dancing to start. She shed her wrap and gave it to Vaughn.

He took it and raised his brow.

"Why do you look that way?" she asked.

He shook his head. "My apologies. You just look... different."

"You *do* look different, actually," Annalies said, studying her frankly with her blue eyes. "Yet nothing has changed."

Natasha smoothed the lace down, suddenly nervous. "Is this inappropriate?" she murmured.

The hoops were very wide, which made her waist look all the smaller. She'd had to cinch in her corset a little to fit into the dress, yet it trimmed her waist in a very satisfying way. The underlayer of the dress was a shimmering silver silk. Over the top of it was the softest layer of white tulle, embroidered with white silk thread in the shape of leaves and flowers and flourishes that followed the hem and each layer of flounce.

The embroidered net had been formed into flowers at her breast, while garlands of the netting finished the low neckline. The tops of her shoulders and her lower arms were bare, for the dress sat around her upper arms. It was the first time in years she had revealed her shoulders. Dancing a reel while wearing long sleeves and a high neck had not seemed sensible.

Elisa, who had the strongest sense of propriety of them all, shook her head. "You are most appropriately and beautifully dressed. It is a delightful gown, Natasha. Perhaps that is the difference? You haven't worn light colors for a long time."

"Yes, that must be it," Anna said in agreement.

Rhys said nothing. He rarely did. His eyes, though, were warmly appreciative. He slid his arm around his wife's waist and Anna rested her hand over his.

"Wraps, coats, hats and gloves, all accounted for," Vaughn said, coming back to join them. "Let's go in and see what the décor is to be, this year."

Finally, Natasha thought, threading her dance card over her wrist.

* * * * *

The dancing was as delightful as ever. Natasha did not lack partners. Even the poor ones who stepped on her toes or hems did not spoil her mood. She wondered why she had ever stopped dancing. There was nothing sinful about dancing, even with near-strangers, and it was such fun!

From time to time during the evening, she found herself looking up at the stairs that led to the entrance to the grand hall. Many years ago, she had first spotted Seth on those stairs and her entire life had changed.

There were just as many observers clinging to the balustrades tonight as there had been that night, while dancers climbed up and down the stairs behind them. None of them were handsome strangers with earrings, though.

She could feel her spirits drooping at the reminder and would force her attention back to the steps and the rhythm of the dance. Each time, the mood passed.

Natasha had not heard of one of the dances before. It was called a flirtatious polka and there was no space next to it on her dance card for a partner to write their name.

Because she had no partner for the dance and because it was new to her, Natasha considered the dance a good opportunity to recover her breath and watch for a while, even though she normally loved the spinning and speed of polkas.

Vaughn, though, had a different idea. He held out his elbow. "Come, lady 'tasha."

"I do not know this dance."

"A simple polka? Of course you do."

"Elisa—"

"Has another partner." He pulled her onto the dance floor and put his hand on her waist. His eye closed in a quick wink. "There is an element to this you may like."

The music began. Vaughn spun her into the first turn and Natasha had no time to talk. Polkas were fast and fun yet she had to concentrate on her steps.

The first movement was nearly complete when Vaughn said warningly, "…and here we go." He spun her and actually let go of her hand.

Natasha drew in a sharp breath, startled.

Another hand landed on her waist, securing her. Her other hand was captured and she was steadied. Natasha looked into Rhys' eyes. He laughed. "You've never danced a flirtation, have you, dear sister?" He spun her into the second movement.

Natasha laughed, too. New dances were introduced each year, often just a simple variation on favorites. This was a delightful variation. Around the dance floor, men were spinning their partners into the waiting hands of the next dancer.

The next partner was an Earl she knew only slightly, yet well enough to enjoy the short moment with him and banter, when she had the breath for it. He turned her into the dizzy movement that would send her into the next man's arms.

The next man was Raymond.

Natasha's breath evaporated. She nearly tripped and Raymond held her up. "You're here!" he breathed. "I did not think you would be. You haven't attended a ball for years." He spun her around.

Natasha couldn't answer. She was too busy dealing with the flurry of thoughts and images in her mind. She had not expected Raymond would attend this ball any sooner than she would. He was still officially in mourning and would be until early September.

His hand on her waist seemed heavy and hot, far more than any other partner tonight. In a few seconds this movement would end and she would be forced to move on.

"Do you have any waltzes left?" Raymond asked quickly.

"One," she admitted.

"Then I claim it," he said, his voice low.

He turned her into the spin and into the arms of the next partner.

Natasha concentrated on smiling and chatting throughout the polka, barely focusing on what she was saying or the movement of her feet. The charm of the dance had dissipated. She waited for it to be over, because there would be an intermission right after it. Given the energetic speed of the dance, she understood why they had scheduled it for just before the pause.

Her last partner was a man she knew only a little. The Duke of Urlingford had direct connections to the Royal Family, and lived a life far above those of the everyday peerage. He was a young man, recently come into his title. Privilege seemed to drip from him.

Natasha was polite. "Good evening, Your Grace."

He was a short man. Even so, his gaze turned downward. He was not looking at her face. "You are the Innesford widow, are you not?" His breath smelled of brandy. There was also a pungent smell of stale tobacco that caught at the back of her throat.

Natasha had to turn herself, for his limp hand gave her no assistance. When she came back to face him, she said breathlessly; "I am Lady Innesford."

"You're more comely than I expected." His eyes, she saw, were bloodshot.

The violins climbed up to the conclusion of the dance

and finished with a quick flourish. The dancers grew still, and clapped wildly. The popularity of the dance was beyond dispute.

The Duke dropped his hand from her waist. His heated gaze roamed over her. Natasha recognized that look. She had seen it on many other men before.

She gave him a quick curtsey. "Your Grace." Then she hurried away, toward the big doors where many of the attendees were streaming through, out onto the balconies for cool air and time to recover.

Natasha found a spot next to the broad stone balustrade and leaned against it, breathing in the fresh air. Compared to the reek emanating from the Duke it was very sweet.

A hand gripped her elbow and yanked her around. The duke glared at her. "I did not dismiss you," he said, his voice low.

Natasha swallowed. It was true that on formal occasions, one did not leave the presence of a duke or royalty until told they could go. A ball, though, was hardly a formal occasion. The waft of brandy warned her to speak carefully.

"I am sorry, your Grace, for my discourtesy. I desperately needed to recover from the vigorous dancing. I was quite...dizzy."

If she had been dizzy, the dancing had not been the cause. The miasmic cigar stench was the more likely source. It was gripping her throat once more. She fought not to wrinkle her nose or gasp.

There were too many people around them for this to be more than a heavy-handed flirtation and she'd had practice at deflecting men from such misjudgments before. It had been a long time since the last occasion, however.

The Duke stepped closer. "Is it true what they say about widows?" he asked.

Natasha swallowed. "What is it do they say, Your Grace?"

"That you're undersexed and hungry."

Natasha caught her breath as his hand gripped her breast and squeezed. She stomped on his foot, only she was wearing dancing slippers and he wore boots. Her foot slid off his protected arch harmlessly.

"Mmm…luscious," he said, his hand working.

"Let go of me!" Her voice was sharp and high, and not by design. This had suddenly and shockingly grown completely out of hand. There were people standing right next to them! True, they had their backs turned as they spoke to their own companions, yet her exclamation made them start and turn to see what was happening in their midst.

The Duke's groping was insistent. Her dress ripped with a low snarling sound and she felt cool air bathe her flesh beneath.

A big hand gripped the Duke's shoulder and turned him. The Duke blinked and looked to see who was trying to interfere with his designs. The movement brought his chin right into the path of Raymond's fist. The punch sounded hard and solid.

The Duke's head snapped back in the other direction and his eyes rolled up.

Raymond caught the Duke as he sagged and lowered

him down to the flagstones and propped him against the balustrade, as everyone around them seemed to make a collective gasp and step back away from them.

Raymond looked up at the nearest man. "Thorsby. Watch the Duke, will you? I must see to Lady Innesford."

"You hit the Duke!" Thorsby breathed, stunned.

"He deserved it. He will remember none of it when he wakes," Raymond said, getting to his feet. He stripped off his coat. "Tell him he passed out from the brandy. It smells as though he has drunk enough of it that the story will hold."

He turned to Natasha, his black eyes passing over her. "You are unhurt?" he asked and draped his coat around her shoulders.

Natasha trembled. The suddenness and speed at which it had happened stunned her. "He...he..."

"Her dress!" someone whispered, their tone horrified.

Raymond pulled the coat together over her shoulders, hiding the ruins of her dress, and looked around the balcony. Then he bent to speak quietly. "The stairs down to the garden are just over there. I'll take you there, rather than through the ballroom, then I'll have one of our carriages brought around."

She nodded, deep relief circling through her. The spectacle she would make, walking through the ballroom in this condition, was more than she could bear.

Raymond caught Thorsby's arm. "You know the Marquess of Farleigh?"

Thorsby nodded.

"Would you find him for me and tell him what has happened? Tell him to bring the carriage around to the back of the garden. Then come back and take care of the Duke."

"Right-oh!" Thorsby hurried off.

Raymond put his arm around her and moved her through the crowd on the balcony. They parted way, letting them through, watching them silently. The whispering started up behind them.

Natasha's trembling worsened. She had become the center of gossip once more.

* * * * *

It was quiet in the garden, with only the sound of crickets and the murmur from the ballroom above them. Light from the ballroom spilled upon the grass. Raymond led her under the trees, along the path to the gate at the back of the garden, and placed her on the bench inside the arbor that covered it.

He sank onto the bench opposite her. The arbor was small, and his knees nearly met hers. He leaned forward. In the moonlight, the white sleeves of his shirt under the brocade vest glowed, even though the moon was already waning from the full.

"Did he hurt you?" he asked softly.

Her trembling was subsiding, which let her feel the ache in her breast. She brought her hand to her chest, resting it on the broadcloth of his coat. "My…" She cleared her throat.

"How badly?" His voice grew harsher.

"Perhaps only a bruise, that is all," she said quickly. "Do not battle the Duke, Raymond. He was drunk, yes, but his family are too powerful to tangle with. Not over me."

"If not you, then who?" he asked. The hard note in his voice did not subside. "Men like him think they are allowed such abuses because no one calls them on it."

"That is true," she said softly. "If that is your reason, Raymond, then I cannot gainsay it. However, I would rather not be just an excuse."

He shot to his feet and walked a tight circle on the path, pushing his hand through his dark hair. "You misunderstand me," he said softly. He stepped back into the arbor and sank down in front of her, until he was looking at her directly. The silk and lace of her dress draped around his boots, yet he didn't seem to notice. "I could have cheerfully killed him when I saw what he was doing to you, and hang the consequences." He cupped her cheek. His hand was warm and large and a shiver rippled through her at his touch. "You are infinitely more important to me than a sodden duke of the realm."

Natasha breathed in every tiny impression of his hand against her. She may even have turned her face into it. Was that how it happened? She didn't know. She only knew that they seemed to draw closer to each other.

Her breath came more quickly as she realized what was about to happen.

Raymond's hand moved against her cheek. He slid it back, to hold her head, telling her exactly what he intended.

"Tell me to stop," he said, his voice very low. "Tell me you don't want this. I will not have you hate me, after."

"I won't hate you," she whispered. It was the truth.

He groaned and kissed her.

His lips were firm and tasted so sweet. His kiss was heady, stealing her breath and every thought in her mind. Her body came alive, every nerve crawling with desire. It had been so long! Oh, how she craved this...

How she had craved Raymond's touch.

Confusion swamped her and Natasha gasped against his lips.

Raymond let her go instantly. "I'm sorry," he said roughly.

"No, don't apologize. I knew what you intended..." Something caught at her throat and squeezed and her eyes pricked with tears, making her vision swim. "It's just that... you are the first man and that was the first kiss since... Seth..." She hung her head, misery swamping her. "I feel as if I have just betrayed him," she whispered.

Raymond made a rough sound and picked her up. He cradled her against him and rested her head on his shoulder. "That was my first kiss since Rose," he said roughly. She could feel his voice rumbling against her. "It is sitting in my chest, making me feel sick and giddy at once," he added.

"*Yes*," she said, gripping his waistcoat lapel. "Exactly that." Hot tears, that made her eyes and her throat ache, dripped onto his shoulder.

He soothed her silently. That was where Elisa and Anna found her barely a minute later. They swooped upon her, asking a dozen anxious questions.

Raymond answered them. "Her dress is torn and she has bruises, but I suspect it was the shock of the moment that has upset her more. Natasha did nothing to justifying the attack. I saw it all."

The clop of horses and the hiss of carriage wheels on the cobbles beyond the gate alerted them to the arriving carriage. Elisa opened the gate and Raymond got to his feet, bringing Natasha with him.

"Let's take you home," he told her.

"Our home," Elisa said firmly. "Natasha should not be alone tonight."

Chapter Seven

Elisa closed the bedroom door softly. Natasha had finally fallen asleep, although for a long time she had laid silently, as shivers wracked her.

Annalies touched Elisa's shoulder, drawing her attention. Then she nodded behind Elisa.

Elisa turned. Raymond was sitting in the upright chair against the passage wall, his shirt sleeves rolled up. He was hunched forward, his arms on his knees, his heel tapping softly.

Annalies held out his coat to him.

"Is she asleep?" Raymond asked, getting to his feet. "Thank you, Aunt Anna." He took the coat and draped it over his arm and tackled the sleeves, unrolling them.

"Asleep, yes, although it took her simply ages," Elisa said.

"That is hardly a surprise," Anna said softly.

"Is she hurt?" he demanded.

"Bruising, that is all," Elisa assured him. She frowned, studying him. "Is there something between you and Natasha, Raymond?"

He finished unrolling his sleeve then looked at her. "Why would you ask that?"

"You saw everything that passed between the Duke and her. Were you watching her?"

"I happened to be on the balcony, that is all. That dress of hers stands out, especially in moonlight. And she cried out, too."

"Oh dear," Anna murmured.

"When she screamed, I had to act." He shrugged and slid the coat on and rearranged the collar. "Natasha is family. I should stand by and let her defend herself against that bastard?"

"Raymond!" Elisa said, shocked. "He is the Duke of Urlingford. You cannot challenge him. He would ruin you. All of us."

"That is what Natasha said," Raymond replied, scowling.

"Then listen to her if you will not take your mother's advice," Elisa shot back. "For now, it was a simple contretemps that can be passed off as a misunderstanding. If you confront the Duke, then it cannot be ignored."

Raymond met her gaze. His expression was flinty. "I have yet to hear a reason why I should do nothing more about this."

Anna squeezed Elisa's elbow, and Elisa swallowed her protest and let Anna speak.

"Raymond, you must see how this will look to others," Anna said. "To the *ton*. You are the son of a friend of hers. You have no legal right to defend her."

"Is that what Rhys will say?" Raymond asked her.

"I am sure of it. Do ask him yourself, though, Raymond," Anna said, not unkindly.

"Besides," Elisa added quickly. "If you respond in any way, you will be keeping the gossip alive. Every day people talk about it is yet another day Natasha will be embarrassed to be seen by anyone."

Raymond hesitated for the first time and Elisa realized that was where he was vulnerable; Natasha herself.

A tight band of worry squeezed Elisa's chest. "What is Natasha to you, Raymond?" she said softly. "Is there more to this than shows?"

Raymond was fussing with his coat sleeves, which looked odd without shirt cuffs beneath them. He finally looked at her. "What if there is?" he asked, his voice low.

Elisa pressed her hand against her chest. "Please tell me you have crossed no line with her, that it is nothing more than…than simple…Oh, Raymond, tell me this is just a passing fancy. Please."

Surprise crossed his face. "You are afraid, Mother? *You*?"

"Oh, you don't know how dangerous it would be to become involved with someone like Natasha. The *scandal*…"

Annalies patted her shoulder. "Natasha is a widow, Raymond. She is already notorious in certain circles, because of Seth's past. If she were to take up with a younger man, it would be the end of her reputation. Yours would not survive, either, and both of you have children you must think of. Their futures depend on your social standing."

"Listen to her," Elisa begged him. "Annalies has experienced this, too."

Anna nodded. "Do you know what they call my marriage to Rhys?"

Raymond considered her for a moment. "No," he admitted. "However, they would not gainsay you to my face. Everyone knows how close our families are."

"They call it a left-handed marriage," Anna said. "It is only because the Queen is grateful for what Rhys did to help save my uncle from being accused of murder that we have any standing in society at all. It is a grudging admittance."

"An admittance I have heard you say many times you would be just as happy to live without," Raymond replied.

"That is because Anna made a choice," Elisa said. "We have all made choices. Are you giving Natasha a choice? Is she aware of the dangers, too?"

Raymond looked away from her. His hands hung in loose fists by his sides, and Elisa knew he was restraining himself. Finally, he looked back at her. His expression was bleak. "You courted social disaster when you married Vaughn, Mother. He is younger than you. Did you think your example would be lost upon me?"

He turned and walked away, anger trailing behind him like steam clouds.

Anna squeezed Elisa's arm once more. "He has a point," she said gently. "We can hardly lecture him on inappropriate alliances when we have made such dangerous matches ourselves."

Elisa fumed, too. "I don't want my children *following* my example!" she said. "I want them to learn from me and avoid the mistakes I made."

"Marrying Vaughn was a mistake?" Anna asked gently, as they moved down the passage after Raymond.

Elisa sighed. "No. Never," she admitted. "Not in twenty

-two years have I ever thought it anything other than the sweetest moment of my life. Every year since then has only made it better."

"Perhaps that is what you should think of the next time you talk to Raymond," Anna suggested.

"If he deigns to speak to me at all," Elisa added, her heart lurching unhappily.

"Perhaps Rhys and Vaughn will be able to make him see sense?" Anna suggested.

Elisa relaxed. "Yes. Of course. Raymond will listen to Vaughn. He always has."

When they reached the drawing room, Vaughn and Rhys were already there. So was Raymond. While the two older men stood at the table where the brandy decanter was located, Raymond had flung himself into the club chair. He was not happy.

"Oh, good, Vaughn…" Elisa said, moving over to him. "Perhaps you and Rhys could explain to Raymond about how foolish it would be to become involved with anyone inappropriate—"

"Like Natasha?" Rhys asked, swirling his brandy.

Annalies stopped at his side, her simple gown swishing about her toes.

Elisa glanced from Rhys to Vaughn.

Vaughn nodded. "Raymond just told us."

"That explains the brandy," Annalies said quietly.

"Told you what, exactly? He would explain nothing to me," Elisa said. She glanced at Raymond. "Do feel free to contribute, Raymond."

"I have said all I am going to say, Mother."

"You've shown consideration and restraint over this Susanna woman for years. Why would you now recklessly involve yourself with another unsuitable match?" Elisa asked him.

"Why is it unsuitable?" Rhys asked curiously.

"Because it is!" Elisa shot back.

"Who is Susanna?" Vaughn asked, startled.

"Actually, there is no legal reason to deny the match," Rhys said. "There are no consanguinity issues."

"You're Natasha's brother," Elisa said. "Does it not bother you in the slightest that Raymond…" She trailed off.

"That I what, Mother?" Raymond asked curiously.

"As we seem to be counting degrees of separation, I should point out that I am only Natasha's half-brother," Rhys said. "And I merely said there was no *legal* reason to prevent an association. Social and familial concerns are another matter and one that Anna and I have no say in."

"Yes, you do," Vaughn said sharply. "Natasha is a blood relative, so there's that. Friendship is another."

"I am a commoner. What I think is irrelevant," Rhys said.

"That is what the *ton* would say," Elisa told him. "I would like to know what you think."

Rhys shrugged and took a mouthful of the brandy. "With all due respect, Elisa, I fail to see what your concern is. To begin, what exactly are we talking about here? Raymond may simply care for her as a friend. Perhaps even a close friend, yet that still requires no alarm. Even if we are speaking of a different sort of relationship, there is still nothing I can see that is objectionable about it. Would the *ton* really disapprove of a widow and a widower forming an alliance? Natasha is a countess, and the daughter of an earl, Raymond a marquess. Society can't wag their heads over either of them reaching too high or falling low."

"Vaughn?" Elisa said, her heart thudding unhappily.

"I am afraid, my sweet one, that I feel much as Rhys does on this."

"Raymond is your son," Elisa said.

"A courtesy title, only," Vaughn reminded her. He picked up her hand and stroked the back of it. "What are you really objecting to, my lady?"

Elisa knew that low voice of his. Vaughn was being reasonable and charming, because she was not. She squeezed her other hand into a fist. "Natasha is older than him."

"Not terribly much older," Vaughn said. He smiled. "You are the last person who can afford to protest based on that, my love."

Elisa could feel her cheeks heating. "Raymond is my son and Natasha is my best friend," she said hotly. "To think of them together is…is…it isn't natural!"

"Ah, and there is the nub of it," Vaughn said softly.

Elisa sighed. She dropped her gaze to her shoes. "I am being unreasonable," she admitted.

"It's perfectly natural, under the circumstances," Annalies said softly.

"Besides, nothing may yet come of it…whatever it may be," Rhys said. He looked over his shoulder to where Raymond was still sitting in the chair. "I don't suppose you care to help us sort out exactly what your relationship is?"

"Are you asking what my intentions are?" Raymond said, his tone curious.

"I suppose, as Natasha's oldest living relative, that is my right," Rhys admitted. "Do I have reason to ask what your intentions are?"

Raymond got to his feet. "Not yet," he said softly.

"That is a statement rife with innuendo," Vaughn said. "You will not explain yourself, Raymond?"

Raymond took the brandy glass from Vaughn's hand and drained it, then handed it back. "No," he said simply.

Elisa let out a deep sigh. "I am afraid you might get hurt again, if this is allowed to continue," she told him. "Both of you," she added. "Natasha is not as strong as she pretends to be."

Raymond met her gaze. "Natasha will not be hurt by anything I do. I promise you that."

Vaughn was watching her closely. Elisa forced herself to smile at Raymond. "I will still worry. I know how cruel people can be."

* * * * *

Natasha slept until nearly noon. When she woke, she found that Elisa had sent a message to Corcoran, who had sent Mulloy back with clothing and accessories for Natasha to use, as she could not come home in a ruined ball gown.

Mulloy helped her dress and clucked her tongue when

she saw the bruising around Natasha's breast. "All I can say is the Duke must have a powerful hand to do that. Look, there are marks right down under your arm and all."

Natasha lifted her arm to look and winced. "Yes, right in the muscle there," she admitted. "That is the only part that hurts anymore." She took the camisole Mulloy held out. "Is there much fuss, downstairs, about what happened last night?"

"Not that they'd say anything to me, my lady, but no, I can't say there is any sort of fuss that I noticed on my way upstairs."

"Is everyone at home?" Natasha asked carefully. She couldn't ask directly about Raymond.

"Lady Farleigh is here, of course," Mulloy said. "Oooh, is the corset going to dig in?"

"The tender spot is above the corset," Natasha told her. "The boning stopped him from getting his hand any lower, thank goodness."

"I suppose the men of the household have all gone about their business for the day," Mulloy added. "Lady Lillian is upstairs with the children. I didn't see anyone else. Paulson pushed me up the stairs straight away."

Natasha worried silently as she finished getting dressed. She would have to ask Elisa if anything else had happened and hope that Elisa would mention if Raymond had done anything ill-advised last night after she had been brought here.

She made her way slowly downstairs, for she was unable to use her normal hand to hold the railing as she descended, as it hurt too much to grip the rail. She moved to the other side of the stairs and used her left hand. It felt odd and she moved down the stairs carefully.

Paulson was waiting for her at the bottom. "Lady Elisa is writing letters in the library," he told her. "I arranged for some of the soup from lunch to be kept warm for you. Shall I have it put on the dining table?"

"Let me speak to Elisa first, thank you, Paulson. Would you see that Mulloy is taken back to my house, please?"

"Of course, my lady."

Natasha went through to the library. Elisa was sitting at Vaughn's desk, writing swiftly. She rose to her feet as soon as she saw Natasha and smiled as she came toward her. "You look none the worse," she said, stopping in front of her. She was wearing a simple wrapper over her crinolines. That told Natasha that Elisa was not expecting company that afternoon, or intending to go out anywhere herself.

"Thank you for letting me stay the night," Natasha told her. "And for taking care of me."

Elisa's smile warmed. "We must watch out for each other. Isn't that what we agreed, years and years ago?"

"It was," Natasha replied.

Elisa turned back to the desk. "Corcoran has been fussing about making sure you eat something before you leave—"

"Did Raymond challenge the Duke?" Natasha asked, the question pushing out of her. She had to know!

Elisa paused, halfway back to the desk, then slowly turned to face her.

"What is it?" Natasha said quickly, in response to the very strange look on Elisa's face. "What did he do?"

Elisa put her hands together. "Raymond did as you asked. He did nothing to the Duke."

Relief trickled through her. Natasha let out a breath she hadn't been aware she was holding. Then she realized what Elisa had not said. "Did Raymond do…something else, instead?"

Elisa hesitated and Natasha's heart beat a little harder.

"He said…" Elisa began. Then she frowned. "He implied that there was an association between the two of you."

Natasha's breath whooshed out of her again. "He said that?" she said weakly.

"He could hardly deny it," Elisa said. "He hovered outside your room for hours. It took all four of us to convince him he should not go off half-cocked and do something the entire Great Family would come to regret. The only argument that curbed him was that you would suffer if he did." Elisa took a breath and simply looked at her.

Natasha's heart thudded wildly. "Oh…" she murmured, inadequately. "Elisa, I—"

Elisa shook her head. "You do not have to explain anything," she said quickly. "Raymond refused to. He made me promise not to tax you with questions, either." She stepped closer and for the first time Natasha saw that she was paler than usual. "Promise me you will be careful, Natasha. Whatever is between the two of you, it could so easily be used against you. I would die, rather than see either of you hurt again."

Natasha took her hand and squeezed it. "Oh, Elisa, if I could explain any of this, I would, without you having to ask. Only, I am not entirely certain what is happening, either." She squeezed her hand again. "I would not let Raymond suffer, not through anything I do."

Elisa let out a tiny sigh. "I know that," she said. "I am pleased to hear you say it, though." She gripped their combined hands with her free one. "Now I really think you should sit and eat, or Corcoran will burst into tears. Come along." She tugged Natasha into turning and following her back out to the dining room.

Two places had been set for them and Corcoran was pouring tea. He beamed approval as Natasha sat down at the place where the bowl of soup sat steaming. "Thank you, Corcoran," she told him.

When he had withdrawn to his post by the door, Natasha picked up her spoon.

Elisa was studying her, a little frown between her brows.

Natasha lifted her brow.

"I have just realized…" Elisa said. "Now I understand the dress, last night." Then she leaned forward and put her hands over her face and shook her head. "My son!" she breathed into her hands. "Oh, this is going to be so *strange!*"

Natasha put her spoon back down. "Does that not define our whole greater family, Elisa? None of us has ever conformed to normal standards."

Elisa put down her hands and laughed. "No, never," she admitted and picked up her tea. "I suppose we can weather one more scandal. We're so well practiced at it now."

Chapter Eight

There really was no mistaking a Paris street for anything other than Paris, Will reflected, as he and Jack strolled down the *Boulevard de Sébastopol* around nine o'clock. It was their first evening in Paris and the city was as charming as Will remembered it. London streets could be picked up and placed inside any big city or town in Europe and not look out of place, while any street in Paris looked only like what it was; *Une route à Paris.*

"There's no need to look so smug," Jack observed. "Peter will never forgive you for leaving him at the hotel."

"We can't bring him to a club," Will pointed out. "Mother would flay both of us and Peter, too, just because she would be so mad."

"She would not."

"You know very well she would," Will said. "Peter will just have to stay mad at us, instead."

Jack fell silent for a few paces. They touched their hat brims as they passed a pair of French women, walking arm in arm. The women gave them sultry, speculative smiles and Will sighed. "Ah…Paris!"

Jack nodded ahead. "I believe that is the club there, where the lantern is burning. You know, Will, we're both men now. Isn't it about time you stopped being scared of your mother? Elisa hasn't so much as shouted at either of us for years."

"Only because she hasn't found out about…well, lots of stuff," Will said, with a sideways grin.

"Like sneaking off from haymaking last August?"

"Breaking the axle on the cab, in Cornwall."

"*That* was your fault," Jack said.

"You were driving," Will pointed out. "I was… occupied."

"She had sharp elbows and jogged me."

Will laughed. "It might have been one of the horses with a broken leg, instead of the axel and we would never have got away with it the way we did. My point is, Mother has reasons to be mad. She just doesn't know about them and I would rather it stay that way. If we brought Peter with us tonight, he would be so excited about stepping into a French club, he would burst if he couldn't tell *someone* about it. You know the first person he would tell."

"Lilly," Jack concluded grimly.

"Precisely. Lilly isn't exactly…fun, anymore."

Jack sighed. "Sometimes, girls do change like that. I just never expected it of Lilly."

"Here we are," Will said as they reached the canopied section of the sidewalk. A butler-type person stood at the door, watching them as they examined the curtained windows and the discreet sign that announced this was *Le Club Sapphic.*

Will moved toward the door. The butler didn't shift from his position in front of it.

"May we enter?" Will said politely, in French.

"Oh, you don't want to come in," the butler said, with complete confidence.

"I assure you, my friend, we most certainly do," Will replied. "A friend of ours is in there and we need to speak to her. It is of vital importance. When we called at her apartment this afternoon, we were told she would be here, you see. We've actually come all the way from London to see her."

The butler considered Will. "Does your friend have a name?"

"Lady Linnea Keadew." Will was struck by sudden inspiration and added, "She may use the name Susanna. It's a family name."

The butler laughed, his big frame shaking with mirth. He gripped his belly, his fingers digging in.

Jack leaned close. "I only followed about half of that, Will. What did you say to him to make him do that?"

"I have no earthly idea."

They both waited for the man to bring himself back under control. The butler wiped tears of mirth from his eyes and shook his head. "*Linnea* is here."

He took a step sideways as they both moved toward the door, blocking them completely. "You still don't want to come in."

"I understood that," Jack said firmly. He reached inside his coat and pulled out a bundle of Sterling notes. "I'll wager he understands this, too." He held them out to the butler and waved them a little, enticing him to reach for them.

The butler tilted his head, studying Jack. Then he sighed

and took the notes. "I warned you," he said. "Don't say I didn't." He opened the door and murmured to someone inside. Then he opened the door wider to let them through. "On the right. There is a parlor where you can wait. *Linnea* will see you there."

"That's better," Will said, as he and Jack moved through the door. They turned to the right and found themselves in a small room with an even smaller round table and two uncomfortable chairs. A sconce with one candle burning was the only light in the room.

A small man pushed aside a curtain on the other side of the room and stepped under it. Over the man's shoulder, Will saw a quite-normal looking club, with men drinking and playing cards, while women who did not deserve to be called ladies wandered the tables, flirting with them.

The man shoved a hand in his pocket, looking from Jack to Will and back. "Is this some sort of prank?" he asked, his voice light and melodious. "I don't know either of you."

Will's mouth dropped open.

Jack sucked in a shocked breath.

The man was Linnea Donaldson. From her neatly shorn head to her natty white bowtie, waistcoat and tails, to her highly polished boots, she was every inch the debonair man about town.

She backed up a step, her face working with fury. "Who sent you?" she demanded. "Whoever it was, tell them I stayed away. I'm abiding by the agreement." She turned.

"No, no, don't go!" Will said urgently. "We're not here because of your family. We're here about Raymond Devlin!"

She turned on one heel and cocked her head. "Raymond Devlin?" she repeated, sounding shocked.

"You know him, yes?" Jack asked.

"Of course I knew him." She snorted with disdain and it was eerily just as a man would do it. "He used to pull my sashes undone and run away. I would chase him and punch him in the face." Again, the disdainful look down her nose. "He was such a *slow* runner." She looked at them, her eyes narrowing. "Why do you want to speak to me about Raymond? I haven't seen in him in years."

"Well, you see—" Jack began.

Will nudged him.

Jack swallowed his words.

"Raymond's birthday is next month," Will said. "We have been chatting with all his friends from long ago, to see if they could attend a party we're giving, as a surprise for Raymond. However, given your current…circumstances, I doubt you will be interested."

"I have no intention of ever setting foot in England again." Linnea pushed her other hand into her trousers. "How did you find me?"

"Your family's secretary return a letter I sent to you and gave me your Paris address," Will told her. Over her shoulder, the curtain she had walked through was not quite properly drawn. Through the chink he could see that the club was not as normal as he had first thought. Most of the men sitting at the tables were not men.

Linnea frowned. "Freddy is a complete fool," she muttered, then squared her shoulders, under the broadcloth jacket. "One more leak to plug, I suppose." She gave them a stiff smile. "I'm sorry your journey to Paris was wasted, gentlemen."

Another "man" burst through the curtains. "Linden! Hurry up old chap. The game is growing cold." She put her arm on Linnea's shoulder and leaned on her, blinking drunkenly.

"I'm coming," Linnea murmured.

"Just one more question, please," Will said quickly.

She looked back.

"Did Raymond call you Susanna?"

"*Susanna?*" the other "man" repeated and laughed, then hiccupped.

"For Susan," Jack added. "You know, a pet name."

Linnea shook her head in disbelief. "If he had I would have broken his nose, not just bloodied it." She pushed her drunk companion through the curtain, then turned and closed it firmly behind them.

Will jerked his head toward the door and Jack hurried after him. They burst out onto the pavement and hurried up the street, neither of them speaking until they reached the corner.

"Stop, stop!" Jack said breathlessly. He leaned against the wall to recover.

Will propped himself against the bricks, too, and blew out his breath heavily.

"No wonder the butler laughed at us," Jack said.

"Right pair of fools, we must have looked," Will muttered.

The silence built for a moment, as they revived. Around them, the nightlife of Paris was strumming. Like her streets, Paris' night time entertainment was of an altogether different flavor.

"Did you know women did that?" Jack asked.

Will shook his head. "Only, when you think about it, it makes an awful kind of sense. After all, men do it. Together, I mean."

"*Some* men," Jack said darkly.

"I've heard some of them even wear dresses."

Jack turned his head to look at Will in disbelief. "So in Paris, the ladies do it too?"

"We probably shouldn't call them ladies," Will observed.

"Most certainly not. I don't want my nose broken," Jack said fervently.

They both burst out laughing. The last of the unpleasant surprise churning in Will's chest eased.

"Thank heavens we didn't bring Peter with us," Jack said. "Can you imagine the fuss he would have made about *that?*"

Will shook his head. "Paris…" he murmured with a sigh.

* * * * *

For a week, Natasha did not stir from the house. She cancelled all her appointments, which had not been many to begin with. Instead, she spent a lot of time with the twins and Lisa Grace. They were the only three children left in the house and even they were growing up rapidly. Daniel, the next oldest, was at Eton with Neil, who was completing his last year there before going on to Cambridge, where Cian was studying. Lilly, of course, was living with Elisa.

The girls adored having their mother with them and their happiness made Natasha feel guilty. She had always spent as much time with the children as they had seemed to need and they had thrived as a result. Had she been neglecting the girls lately?

To make up for any lack, Natasha told their governess, Adelaide, to take a week's holiday while the weather was so glorious. Natasha took over their lessons for the week, although she was not nearly as rigorous in their application as Adelaide might have been. There was a lot of giggling and simple fun in that week. Corcoran spent most of the week looking upset, as he trailed after the girls, picking up, putting to rights and wiping off smears.

Elisa sent three letters, demanding to know why Natasha had failed to meet appointments they had in common, such as Lady Arrowood's whist afternoon. Natasha wrote back, explaining truthfully that she felt uncomfortable about appearing in public so soon after yet another scandal.

Elisa's third letter was far more direct.

Have you spoken to Raymond since the ball?

Natasha took a day to answer that one. When she did, she prevaricated.

I'm very busy with Lisa Grace, Mairin and Bridget.

She sealed the letter and dropped it on the tray before she could change her mind.

The truth was, every time she thought of Raymond, which was often, she thought of the kiss. It had been hovering near the front of her mind all week. When she relaxed, the moment would slide back into her thoughts and her body would tighten and her heart thud and the ache would return in a rush.

Then she would think of Seth and moan with self-loathing. At night, the empty pillow next to hers seemed to accuse her.

When Elisa wrote for a fourth time, insisting Natasha attend Sarah, Lady Bellfield's at-home the next day, Natasha assured Elisa she would be there. Hiding away in the house was making things worse. She had far too much time to think.

Elisa sent a message saying she would pick Natasha up and take her to Lady Bellfield's herself.

Natasha did not dispute the arrangement. Elisa was merely ensuring that Natasha would arrive as promised. It would be good to have a friend by her side when she finally faced the *ton* once more.

She donned her best afternoon dress. The skirt was a pale blue organza and the jacket was made of three different shades of blue, ranging from the blue of the skirt to a deep, midnight blue. Her bonnet was the same shade as the darkest blue on her jacket.

Elisa's carriage arrived precisely on time. Elisa did not alight to step into the house to collect her. Instead, she remained in the carriage. Corcoran drew Natasha's attention to the waiting vehicle.

"Lady Farleigh means to force me out of the house one way or the other," Natasha told him.

"She is indominable," Corcoran murmured and handed Natasha her bonnet.

Elisa smiled when she saw her. "You look lovely, as usual. That blue matches your eyes."

Natasha settled on the seat next to her and pulled her skirt aside so the footman could close the door. "Is it at all shocking?" she asked anxiously, smoothing the skirt, as the carriage rolled into motion.

"Not in the slightest," Elisa assured her. "I am sure no one blames you for what happened with the Duke, Natasha."

"I can't help but feel it *was* my fault," Natasha said. "For years I have not had a single inappropriate comment or leer. I had grown used to not being seen and had relaxed and enjoyed myself. Then I lowered my dress, uncovered my arms and wore something other than black." She shook her head. "I wish I had remembered how some men seem to think I am something they can play with."

"You had forgotten because Seth was always there. He kept you safe," Elisa said.

"He did. I am only glad Raymond saw what was happening."

Elisa sighed. "So am I."

"Really, Elisa?" Natasha asked her. "I thought you could not cope with the idea."

"I cannot, although I am trying my hardest to find a way." Elisa bit her lip. "If Raymond had not stepped in, though, you would have been far more hurt than you were. For that, I really *am* glad. How are your bruises?"

"They are nearly healed," Natasha said. She glanced out the window and frowned. "Where are we? Is your driver using a different route today?"

"Possibly," Elisa said, glancing out the window. "Tell me how your week of playing with the girls went. Your letters were short on details."

Natasha described the lessons, the games and the silliness of the week. Her gaze was drawn through the window as familiar houses passed by, halting her narrative. "Why, this is…Berkeley Square!" She looked at Elisa accusingly.

Elisa peered through the window for a long moment. "I do believe it is," she said softly and sat back, her gaze ahead.

"Lady Bellfield does not live on Berkeley Square, Elisa," Natasha pointed out. Many of the friends they had in common *did* live on the square, including Raymond. That fact was making her heart beat harder. "Why are we here?" she demanded.

The carriage came to a gentle stop. A quick glance across the road at the houses there confirmed what Natasha suspected. They had stopped at Raymond's house.

"Elisa?" she prompted.

"I grew tired of you hiding away," Elisa said. She waved toward the door as Raymond's footman opened it. "After you."

Natasha stayed where she was. "Did you talk to Raymond again?"

"There have been as few letters from him as from you.

In fact, he has been hibernating here. One might almost say he has been brooding."

Natasha shrank back on the seat. "He has no idea we are here, does he?"

"By now, he will," Elisa said. "Thomsett is a spry young man and won't have dawdled to tell Raymond he is about to have visitors. There is no point in clinging to the seat, Natasha. Out you go." Elisa pushed at her hip.

Natasha's belly cramped. "What about Sarah, Lady Bellfield?"

"I told her we were both indisposed," Elisa said. She pushed again. "My lord, you are a rock, aren't you?"

"I am not," Natasha replied hotly. She rose and stepped out of the carriage, irritable and upset. "How could you do this to me? To Raymond?"

Elisa took her arm and almost dragged her over to the door, where Thomsett stood waiting, holding it open for them. "Inside," she said firmly. "I refuse to discuss this on the pavement as though I were a fishwife shouting her wares."

"Good afternoon Lady Farleigh, Lady Innesford," Thomsett murmured as they stepped inside. "Can I take your things?"

"I won't be staying, Thomsett," Elisa said.

"What is this, Mother?" Raymond said.

Natasha looked over Elisa's shoulder. Raymond was emerging from the library, pulling his coat into place. He must have been working in shirt sleeves. Elisa really had caught him by surprise.

Natasha realized she was staring at him, her gaze moving from toe to tip, taking in every detail. The heavy yearning billowed, making her limbs feel weak and her heart strain. It had only been a week since she had seen him, yet it felt much longer. His thick black hair looked disheveled. Even his dark eyes looked tired. Every time she saw him, she was reacquainted with how tall he was.

She shivered.

Raymond lifted a brow at his mother.

Elisa glanced at Thomsett.

"I believe I am needed in the kitchen," Thomsett said and hurried away.

Elisa waited until Thomsett disappeared, then turned to Raymond. "You are both behaving like small children. Hiding away, licking your wounds because the world frowned upon you. You must have known you courted disapproval, yet you sulk when you receive it. Well, no more. I bought Natasha here today so you can speak in private. You and she must decide what you want, Raymond. Then you must hold up your chins and look the family and the *ton* in the eye." Elisa turned to Natasha. "You did exactly that for me, once. For me and for Vaughn, even though it might have misfired and you would have been a social outcast for doing so. Now, I will do the same for you. Talk to Raymond. Decide what you want. Whatever you decide, whatever it is you want, I will stand by your side for the world to see and support that decision."

She nodded at Raymond and turned to go.

Natasha caught her wrist, as Raymond hurried to open

the door for her.

Elisa looked at her hand, then at Natasha.

"You would do that, even though you do not approve?" Natasha asked.

"My objections are all purely emotional," Elisa said. She looked at them both once more. "I will not be the cause of your unhappiness. There are far too many others you have yet to face who will deliver their own suffering."

She stepped out of the house and over to the waiting carriage and did not look back.

Raymond shut the door, leaving Natasha alone with him.

Chapter Nine

Natasha gripped her reticule. She felt frozen to the spot.

Raymond met her gaze. "Why don't you at least take off your gloves and bonnet? Even if you return home immediately, it will still take some time for the carriage to be ready. You can be comfortable while you wait."

Natasha wasn't sure she wanted to move. She was gripped by a paralyzing mix of conflicting emotions. "I did not know Elisa would do this," she said. Her voice was strained.

"I could tell that when I watched you arrive." He held out his hand. "Give me your purse. Let's begin there."

She hesitated. Yet there was nothing significant about handing over her things. She did it many times a day. She held out the reticule on its cord.

Raymond took that and put it on the sideboard under the big mirror.

It was automatic, after that, to take off her gloves and remove her bonnet. Raymond put both of them next to her reticule. "Now, would you like tea?"

"Something stronger, actually," Natasha admitted.

His smile was small, deepening the line on one side of his mouth. "That sounds like a *very* good idea. I have some madeira—"

"I would prefer brandy." Madeira was a lady's drink.

Raymond's brow lifted again. "Brandy it is, then." He

waved toward the drawing room.

"The library," she said. "The drawing room is too…"

"Formal," he finished and nodded.

Natasha walked over to the recessed doors into the library and stepped inside. This room wasn't nearly as large as Elisa and Vaughn's big archive, yet it had the same sort of warmth. There was something magical about a room filled with books. People who read books, who owned them and cared for them enough to give them a special room were thinkers. Natasha had grown up without one, yet her years with Seth and his habit of reading anything that crossed his path had taught her to appreciate the wealth of knowledge a library held. A library always made her feel comfortable.

She moved over to the pair of dark green velvet armchairs arranged in the corner opposite Raymond's desk and settled in one.

Raymond poured brandy into two snifters and brought them over to the chairs. He placed one on the small round table next to Natasha and sat in the other chair, his snifter in his hand. He crossed his knee over the other. It made him look relaxed. Natasha wondered if that was his true state and glanced again at the dark marks under his eyes.

"How do you fare, Natasha?" he asked. "Are you quite well, now?"

"Well enough. You look tired."

He took a sip of the brandy. "I admit that sleep has not come easily to me lately."

"Because of me?"

He frowned, looked down at the brandy. "Because of

Rose," he said shortly. He met her gaze. "Because I kissed you."

Something shifted in her chest and tension loosened. It was relief. "I have been feeling as though I am the most despicable woman alive," Natasha said softly. She groped for the glass and brought it to her lips.

"Because we enjoyed it," he finished.

Natasha nodded and met his gaze once more. "Why did you tell the family about…us?"

"I only told them that I was involved with you in some indeterminate way. I was not indiscreet, Natasha."

"I didn't think you were," she assured him. "Yet I thought we had agreed that our friendship should remain a secret."

"From the *ton*, yes," Raymond replied. "However, that moment with the Duke told me we will need allies, going forward. We will need safe haven. The family can provide both. I wanted to test their tolerance, to see if they could accept the idea of a possible liaison."

Her heart jumped. "We have only spoken of being friends…"

Raymond's gaze wouldn't let her go. "What we have spoken of barely begins to plumb the depths. You know that as well as I. It is in your face as we speak, right now."

Natasha dropped her gaze to her brandy. The glass was empty. She had not noticed how she had gulped it. She put the glass back on the table and rubbed her hand where the sharp edges of the crystal had dug furrows. "You said you would not force the issue, that I could set the terms."

"I did not lie."

"Is that why you have stayed away for a week?" she asked, able to look at him once more.

His gaze was steady. "I needed to sort things out in my own mind, before I saw you again. I have trouble thinking when you are in the room, you see."

Her heart squeezed and her body tightened. She swallowed. "Even now?'

"As my mind is settled now, I can sit here and enjoy your beauty."

Natasha could feel her cheeks growing warm. Many men had told her she was beautiful. Raymond, though, made it sound profound and moving, that he really *did* think she was beautiful and only wanted to appreciate that and not possess her, as the Duke of Urlingford had.

She touched her hair self-consciously. Until this moment, the white streak that had appeared there a few years ago, running from her temple, had not bothered her. Many ladies mourned their youth when they spotted gray in their hair and would beat their chests and despair. Just not her.

Until now.

"That only makes you uniquely beautiful," Raymond said.

"It makes me look old."

"It makes you look like a woman who has lived," Raymond assured her. "That is a prize no debutante can offer."

She realized she was trying to hide the streak with her hand and lowered it back to her lap. "It just appeared overnight," she confessed.

"When Seth died," Raymond added.

She jumped. "How did you know that?"

"I saw it appear, too."

"You noticed that?"

"I did." He shifted, putting both boots on the floor and the empty glass to one side. "Shall we agree on something, Natasha? Shall we agree that we are both free to speak of those we have loved who have gone?"

Natasha drew in a shaky breath. "You would not mind?"

"Seth was part of you. He is still a part of you. No, I don't mind. I would encourage it. You loved him. It has made you who you are and I would know all of you, if you will let me."

Natasha met his gaze once more. "And will you tell me about the woman you loved?"

"Rose?" he asked, puzzled.

"Susanna."

His jaw flexed. "Susanna is not gone yet."

"For you, she may as well be," Natasha replied. "Rose inspires guilt in you when you kiss me, because she died. I think it is Susanna, though, who has prevented you from sleeping and put those marks under your eyes."

"You are right," he said. "But not for the reasons you think. I will tell you about Susanna one day. I promise you I will. For now, though, I cannot, for the same reasons I refused to give anyone in the family details about you."

He had refused because he was honorable and had given his word. Discretion was a part of his marrow, Natasha realized. In that, he was just like his mother. She would have to remember to point out to Elisa exactly how much Elisa had influenced her son.

There was clearly a similar impediment preventing Raymond from telling her about Susanna, even if he wanted to, which he said he did. It would be unfair to probe any further. "Very well," Natasha said. "I will not ask about her again."

Raymond raised a brow. "Thank you," he said. "Tell me about Seth."

"You know all there is to know," Natasha said uneasily. "He returned from a voyage to Australia with a fever. Blackwater fever. He didn't recover."

"And neither did you," Raymond added.

She suddenly wished she had another glass of brandy. "It hurts, to speak of him."

"Of course it does. Only, when you *do* begin to speak of him, you censor yourself because you think I will object to the idea that you loved and lived with another man before me. I would stop you from feeling that way, if I can."

"Can you stop me from feeling wretched because I like kissing you?" she asked.

Raymond's eyes widened.

Natasha drew in a sharp breath and looked down at her hands once more.

"No, look at me," Raymond insisted.

She lifted her chin.

He shifted to the front of his chair and leaned forward. "We both recoil for the same reason," he said softly. "Even though we both enjoyed it." He linked his hands together. It looked like a casual movement, yet his fingers whitened as he gripped them. "Tell me, Natasha, if you could kiss me and *not* feel that guilt, would you want to?"

"You mean, simply kiss you and enjoy it?"

"Yes."

A moonlight night and lace curtains, flittered through her mind, which stirred her innards once more. To feel that pleasure and not be alone… She gathered her courage and said, "Yes, I would want that."

"Then I think we should practice, until we have it."

Her pulse leapt. "P-practice?"

"Repeat the behavior until the desired result is achieved."

"Then, that is what you want, too?"

"More than you could possibly know," he said, his voice low.

Her heart seemed to throw itself against her chest. "How does one go about practicing…um, kissing?"

"I imagine, the same way one practices bowling by bowling. Shall we?" The corner of his mouth was lifting again. She liked the way his smiles always seemed to emerge reluctantly from him, as if he was being pulled into good humor instead of merely expressing it. It made his smiles seem far more genuine than the hollow expressions she sometimes saw at society events.

He got to his feet and held out his hand. "Stand up," he said.

She took his hand. Even that simple touch made her fingers tingle. When she was standing, she said: "I think you should take off your jacket. Men always practice in shirt sleeves."

His smile was complete this time. He shrugged out of the coat. "I have always thought it monstrously unfair that ladies must clean, cook, sew and garden while wearing every layer, with not a button out of place, while men are free to cast aside all but their undershirts in the name of sports." He laid the coat over the back of the chair and turned back to face her.

Natasha stepped closer to him and he grew still.

"I would like to…" she began and rested her hands against his forearms. She curled her fingers around them, feeling the thick muscle and the heat through the linen of his shirt. Slowly, she ran her hands up his arms, learning the shape of them and accustoming herself to touching a man who was not Seth. It made her tremble with her own daring, yet she forced herself to keep going. She rested her hands on his shoulders for a moment, adjusting to the higher reach.

Then she realized she was censoring herself again. "You are taller than Seth was," she made herself say.

"I watched Seth haul in wet sails, once. He did it one-handed, while hanging from rigging with the other. Height does not mean everything," Raymond said.

Natasha looked at him, surprised. "Yes, he was very strong," she said. "I imagine you are, too. You have the shoulders and the arms."

"I do well enough," he said, although she could hear his amusement. Then she remembered that he had knocked the

Duke of Urlingford unconscious with one blow. Yes, he was strong.

Natasha realized she was putting the moment off. Deliberately, she slid her arms around Raymond's neck. She had to reach to do so. Then she turned her mouth up to his and pressed her lips against him.

For a moment, she could feel nothing but trembling and a sick weakness that made her want to tear herself away from him.

Then he gave a soft, ragged exhalation, as if he were holding onto the last ends of his restraint. Her body seemed to snap to tautness at the sound. Every inch of her came alive. Her limbs developed a limp heaviness and she could feel her heart pounding in her head and her throat. The flesh between her legs pulsed with the same frantic beat. Her breasts swelled inside the corset and rubbed against the camisole.

Raymond's hands curled around her waist, then slid around behind her. She thrilled as he pulled her more tightly against him. They were sandwiched together, from breast to thighs and he was hot and hard against her.

Oh, it had been so long since she had been held like this! She had missed it and not known what she missed.

Seth…!

Natasha pushed herself away from Raymond and he let her go. He was breathing hard, his eyes narrowed, yet he said nothing.

She pressed her hand to her chest, her breath too quick and deep. Her corset was limiting her to little pants. She felt chilled down her front where he had been pressed against her.

Natasha straightened. She wanted to enjoy that feeling again. "Once more," she said.

Raymond drew her to him, pulling her right up against him just as she wanted and she let out a shaky breath. "It is so good to be held again," she whispered.

"It is so good to hold you." His lips brushed her mouth, then pressed against her.

There was very little resistance, this time. Natasha held herself still until it passed, then let herself sink into the pure joy of the kiss. His lips were firm against hers. His hands smoothed along her back, moving restlessly. One moved up to hold her head and the kiss deepened. His tongue probed her mouth, plying against her lips and teeth, then stroking her tongue.

Against her, she could feel his swelling excitement. Pleasure rippled through her and her nub tingled. She grew damp between her legs. Suddenly, she wished that none of the layers between them were there. Then this thrill that she was feeling could be extended and increased, with no barriers for his hands or mouth, or for hers.

She could so easily see herself exploring every plane and facet of him. She moaned at the idea.

Raymond grew still. He lifted his mouth away and rested his forehead against hers. They were both breathing heavily.

"No guilt?" he murmured.

"Not now," she whispered back.

"Nor I."

Natasha stepped away from him. It felt as though even her feet were pulsing with the heated need racing through her. "I must go," she said.

"You must?" He made no move to prevent her.

"I must walk. I have far too much energy to stand still. I will walk home."

"I will escort you home."

"Thank you, but you are the reason for the energy. If you were to go with me, it would not help in the slightest."

"Very well," he said as she walked out to the front hall-way. "Mayfair is safe enough in the middle of the day. Only, I want you to send a note when you are home."

She tied her bonnet quickly and pushed her hands into the gloves. "I will."

Raymond held out her reticule. She took it, then reached up and pressed her mouth to his once more. Raymond caught her head and held it, his fingers tangling in the ties to her bonnet. He kissed her more thoroughly than she had intended, yet she enjoyed it, all the same.

She was breathless once more when she stepped out of the door. She did not fully get her breath back until she was home, because all the way back to Park Lane, thoughts of what it would be like to be held by him when garments were not a barrier left her dazed and her heart working far harder than a simple stroll demanded.

Chapter Ten

"I know the two of you are lying," Lilly told Will and Jack. "What is it you are not telling me?"

The men exchanged glances. Guilt poured from them in awkward waves, as they shifted their feet. Lilly had seen Elisa's children do the same thing. It was almost amusing, watching two grown men squirm, for they were standing in the middle of the room where Lilly conducted her lessons. The tables and chairs were all child-sized, making Will and Jack look larger than normal.

Jack tugged at the brim of the hat in his hand. "We've said all we can say," he mumbled. His coal black, curly hair and beard were such a contrast to Will's sandy hair and green eyes, yet the two of them were closer than real brothers and inclined to mischief. Lilly didn't for a moment think they had been candid.

"What happened in Paris?" she asked, putting her hands on her waist, even though it was not ladylike. "What sort of trouble did you get into?"

"No trouble," Will said quickly. "We spoke to Lady Keadew, who said she wasn't Susanna." He shrugged.

"Yet she knows Raymond," Lilly clarified.

"Not for years, though," Jack said.

"And you believed her?" Lilly asked. "Just like that?"

Again, the two of them exchanged glances.

"What made you think she was telling the truth?" Lilly pressed.

"Believe me, if you had seen her, you would not have doubted her," Jack said.

Will shoved his elbow in Jack's side.

"Why would I not have doubted her? What did she look like?" Lilly demanded.

Even Will, who was a slightly better liar than Jack, looked ill at ease.

"Come, come," Lilly snapped. "You've said too much now. Out with it. Tell me everything."

"It's just that…it's shocking," Will said.

"I haven't been shocked since you told me Father Christmas was not real," Lilly shot back. She waited.

Jack cleared his throat. "Well…we got to Paris late in the afternoon, you see…" Gradually the story emerged. A club, a large butler and a rather smaller "man". Lilly sank down onto the chair behind her desk, staring at them. She took off her spectacles and cleaned them on a fold of her walking suit, unable to meet their eyes.

When their tale was done, she put her hands on the desk, one over the other. "She may very well be Susanna," she said slowly.

"She can't be!" Will protested. "She isn't the type to be interested in men at all."

"All the more reason for Raymond to stay away from her and not tell a soul a thing about her," Lilly pointed out.

Jack drew himself up to his full height and crossed his arms. "I don't believe it," he said flatly. "Raymond has too much self-respect to fall for a lady—a *woman* like that."

"The heart is strange, sometimes," Lilly told them. "It is contrary. The more an admirer is pushed away and rejected, the more they obsess about the object of their affection."

"That still doesn't sound like Raymond," Will pointed out.

"Besides, she said she wasn't called Susanna by anyone," Jack added.

"Maybe Raymond only calls her that in his most private thoughts," Lilly said.

"Except now the whole family knows about Susanna, doesn't it?" Will said.

"We know *of* Susanna. We don't know who she is for certain," Lilly said. She got to her feet. "You must keep investigating. Come back and tell me what you find."

The two stared at her.

She waved them away. "Go on. Shoo. I have to get the girls ready for supper."

* * * * *

Raymond kissed Natasha seventeen times over the next week. She had not intended to keep count, yet each kiss lingered in her memory, a small event on its own.

The very evening of the first kiss in his library, Raymond arrived unannounced on her doorstep, wearing evening clothes and a cape. Corcoran merely raised his brows. "Viscount Marblethorpe."

"I would speak to Natasha for only a moment," Raymond began, then his gaze shifted to where Natasha stood at the door to the dining room. "About the Orphans Society," he added.

"You had better come in," Natasha said, fighting to keep her voice calm. Her heart was racing, though. Her body was tingling.

Corcoran took Raymond's hat. Raymond didn't remove the cape. "I really am staying only a moment," he said.

"Very good, my lord."

Natasha walked into the library. Raymond followed her in. The room seemed to shrink around him. He came right up to her, despite the open door behind him. His gaze met hers. "Tell me," he said quietly. "Today, after the library, when you got home, did you fret about Seth?"

Her mouth parted. "Yes," she said, breathing out her surprise. "You, too? I mean—"

He kissed her, halting her words, stealing her breath and robbing her of thought. His arm came around her. She was very nearly lifted off her feet for he held her tightly against him. The cape came around them, enclosing her in his arms and his warmth.

It was not a short kiss. When he let her go at last, he held her steady until her knees worked once more. She pressed her fingers to her lips. They were swollen.

"There. That's better," he murmured.

She nodded.

He kissed her cheek and left.

She tossed sleeplessly that night and several times realized her hand was fluttering against her hip, or absently stroking her thigh as she recalled the details of the two kisses so far. She would roll onto her side and tuck her hand under the pillow, to remove temptation.

Deliberately, she would study the empty pillow next to her.

She could not sit still the next morning. She put on a walking suit and crossed Park Lane to Hyde Park far earlier than was customary to walk the paths alone, her heart hurrying along. By the time she felt that she might have exercised enough to remain in ladylike repose for the rest of the day, the paths had filled with all manner of people, most of them friends and acquaintances. The ride was filled with open carriages and people on horseback, cantering in the fresh morning air.

One of them was Raymond. Natasha caught her breath when she saw him. He had not seen her yet. Normally, she would not consider flagging down a rider. It would look presumptuous and cause a fuss. This morning, though, she lifted her hems and hurried over to the edge of the ride, then hesitated on the very brink. Should she wave? Call out? She was already well beyond polite behavior and had no idea.

Raymond resolved the puzzle. He cantered the horse over to where she stood and jumped out of the saddle with an easy movement that drew attention to his long legs and powerful thighs.

Natasha's heart had already been hurrying along. Now it tripled its pace and she swallowed hard.

Raymond drew the horse along behind him by the reins and walked next to her for a mile or more, talking politely, as many others in the park were doing. At the end of the ride, he glanced around to check for observers. Using the stallion as a shield, he pulled her into his arm and kissed her, as she had been hoping he would do since she had seen him.

Then, with a smile that said he knew the state he was leaving her in, he jumped back onto the gray and rode off.

Natasha's hopes that she could calmly move through her day had been utterly annihilated.

One of the things Raymond had mentioned while they were walking was that he had an afternoon appointment with Rhys, on a legal matter. Natasha had visited Rhys in his offices more than once. She had Cook pack up some of her strawberry preserves in a basket and walked to Chancery Lane. There, she put the basket over her arm and sailed into Rhys' office without knocking.

"Dear brother…" She stopped and glanced at Raymond, who had been sitting in the chair in front of Rhys' big desk. "I've interrupted," she added, as both men jumped to their feet.

Rhys looked from her to Raymond. "Yes, you have interrupted," he said slowly. Suspiciously.

Natasha held the basket out to him. "For Anna. I know how she likes them. You should find a cool, dark place for them, so they don't spoil."

Rhys looked into the basket. "I didn't think preserves *could* spoil."

Raymond made no attempt to help Natasha with the bluff. He simply watched her.

Rhys cleared his throat. "I should find somewhere to put

these," he said, moving to the door. "It may take me a few minutes," he said, looking at them.

"I'm happy to wait," Raymond said blandly.

Rhys shut the door behind him.

The door had barely closed before Raymond pulled her to him and bent her over his arm. Natasha rested her hand against his chest. She could hear his heart beating. Then she slid her arm over his neck and kissed him.

By the time Rhys had returned, they were apart once more and Natasha had nearly recovered her breath.

The next kiss happened at the opera house, barely out of sight of any observers. Raymond pulled her out of her box and into the corridor beyond. He pressed her up against the wall, hidden only by the deep sweep of a fringed velvet swag. He kissed her, his hands roaming over her bodice, yet not quite reaching her breasts, which ached for his touch. When she had been reduced to a quivering, mindless wanton, he let her mouth go and dropped his lips to her décolletage.

Her whole body shuddered in delight as his heated lips pressed against her upper breast.

Each kiss seemed to grow more brazen, the risks they took rising to match Natasha's growing frustration. Once, Raymond even kissed her right out in the open, on Berkeley Square, when a momentary lull in traffic gave him the opportunity. Only the fact that nearly everyone in society was at Cowes for the sailing regatta saved them from being observed by any of the number of people they knew who also lived in Berkeley Square.

There were two kisses in her dining room. Another that he stole in the front hall of Elisa's townhouse, when everyone was moving from the dining room to the drawing room after dinner.

Many of the kisses arrived the same way as the second; Raymond would appear on her doorstep, sweep into the house, press her against whatever wall was nearest and kiss her into trembling helplessness, then with a small smile, he would leave again. Sometimes he said nothing at all.

When she went too long without a kiss, Natasha would take her own the same way. She would walk or take the carriage to Berkeley Square and step into the house with a nod to Thomsett, who would quietly tell her where to find Raymond. She would try to push Raymond against a wall. It was a gesture only. He was steady on his feet and disinclined to be moved around by anyone. The symbol was enough, though, for him to pick her up and kiss the breath from her.

Natasha's sleep became a tortured wasteland. She refused to indulge herself as she had that moonlit night. Instead she would lie awake, wondering if she dared take the next, perfectly obvious step. They had already taken so many risks, it didn't seem to be such a giant leap. Yet, to take the step would close a gate behind them. There would be no going back.

Her walks in Hyde Park each morning became more protracted, as she strove to exorcise some of the tension that never properly disappeared anymore, not even when Raymond's kisses were more than a day apart.

When everyone had returned from Cowes and were preparing for the Glorious Twelfth, that marked the end of the London Season, the paths and rides filled up once more with all the usual people. On the tenth of August, though, Natasha ran into Morven, Lady Tachbrook. The dark haired woman smiled a wary greeting. "Lady Innesford."

"Natasha, please," Natasha told her. After her conversation with Raymond about the sexual practices of people like Morven, all Natasha felt for the woman was pity. She had suffered through a lonely life, after all. Natasha knew what that sort of soul-empty loneliness felt like. "Walk with me," she told Morven. "Just for a moment or two. How is it you are in London? I thought you did not wish to remain for the season?"

"I did go back to Inverness," Morven admitted. "Social obligations forced me to return to London. If I can manage to avoid any further commitments while I am here, then I will be able to remain in Scotland after the twelfth."

Natasha saw Raymond approaching from the corner of her eye. She could find him among the crowded footpaths with ease, now. He was walking this morning and took off his hat as he approached her, his gaze flicking toward Morven. "Lady Innesford," he said, with formal politeness. There was almost a chill in his voice.

"Lord Marblethorpe, do you know Morven, Lady Tachbrook, of Inverness?"

Raymond gave Morven the shortened bow, that was very nearly a mere nod of the head, that was all that was required of a high-ranked gentleman meeting a lady of lesser rank. "Lady Tachbrook," he murmured.

"A pleasure, my lord," Morven replied. She smiled easily and prettily. "It is a lovely morning, isn't it?"

"It was," Raymond replied. He pulled out his watch and consulted it. "Unfortunately, I must return home at once. A matter has arisen. Lady Tachbrook, Lady Natasha." He did bow, this time, and only to Natasha.

Puzzled, Natasha watched him stride away, moving fast and weaving between strollers. "How odd," she murmured.

"Did I interrupt an assignation?" Morven asked, the same amused smile still in place.

Natasha regarded her coolly. The first time Morven had tried to shock her with her ribald conversation had worked only because Natasha had been ignorant. Now, she knew better. "There was no assignation," she said blandly.

"You seem rather friendly with Marblethorpe."

"We are family," Natasha said, letting the chill creep into her voice. "Actually, I have an early appointment of my own to keep. Please excuse me, Lady Tachbrook."

She hurried away, before Morven could even acknowledge her departure. They were at the far end of the park, while Natasha's house was halfway along the length of it. She stepped out of the park and crossed Park Lane to walk along the footpath beside the houses that overlooked the park. It was not nearly as pleasant a walk as the park paths were, only she had lost interest in pleasing vistas.

Morven had reminded her that the risks she and Raymond were taking could have severe consequences. Morven was not the only person who understood the sexual under-layers of society, that hid behind propriety.

Natasha hurried up the steps and into the house. She caught Corcoran off guard for once—he was nowhere to be seen. That suited her mood. She hurried up the stairs to her bedroom before anyone could see her face.

She hurried into the bedroom, already unpinning her hair.

"How do you know that woman?" Raymond asked.

Natasha jumped and muffled her scream against her hands, spinning to look behind her.

Raymond had been sitting in the rocking chair in the corner. He got to his feet, making the room shrink.

"Oh, my dear sweet lord!" Natasha said, her voice muffled by her hands. Her voice wobbled. She had been badly frightened. She was shaking with it, her heart thrumming fast. "What on earth do you think you are *doing* here, Raymond?" She spoke quietly. The upstairs maids would still be working on the bedrooms on this side of the house.

"It was the first place I could think of where we could talk and be guaranteed no interruptions." He kept his voice down, too.

"Did Corcoran let you up here?" She pushed her loose hair over her shoulder. Her hands trembled and it took two tries.

"He doesn't know I am here." Raymond came toward her. She held up her shaking hand. He halted at the foot of the bed.

She grabbed the brass bed post on the other side and bent over, trying to draw a deep enough breath. Her stays were too tight.

"I have frightened you," he said softly. "I apologize. That was not my intention."

"You didn't think I would be startled to find *anyone* in here?" she demanded. It took two breaths to say it.

"I barely thought beyond the need to speak to you about *her*."

Natasha could at last draw a deep enough breath. She straightened and looked at him. "Morven Fortescue? What of her? She is barely an acquaintance."

"She is the one who upset you with her frank talk about affairs and sex, is she not?" Raymond asked. "I understand far more clearly now I have seen her. You said she was a peer?"

"Her husband was Baronet Tachbrook, from northern Scotland."

"She *says* that is who she is, only are you sure?" Raymond asked. "Has anyone vouched for her?"

"Lady Gaddesby, the President of the London Orphan Society, introduced Morven." Natasha took another deep breath. Her trembling was subsiding. "Lady Gaddesby is not a fool. She would not open her arms to anyone who did not have a solid reference. Raymond, what is this? Why are you so suspicious of Morven Fortescue?"

Raymond looked away. "Then she is a true blue blood," he murmured, almost to himself. He moved closer and his voice dropped even lower. "You cannot see or speak to her any further, Natasha. You must cut her dead."

"Cut her... Raymond, why on earth must I be so rude? I do not understand."

"I cannot explain it further. You must trust me on this. Do not speak to her." His gaze met hers. "Promise me."

"No," Natasha said. "Not without reason. Not without *good* reason. Your mother went through eight years of purgatory because too many people were willing to act upon pure gossip. I refuse to do the same."

Raymond grew still. "This is not the same thing at all. I have every good reason to insist upon this."

"You...*insist?*" she repeated. Her chest grew hot and hard.

His eyes narrowed. "You will refuse me?" he asked, his voice dangerously low.

The curse rose to her lips without thought. "Until kangaroos fly and dingoes talk, mate." Even the drawl was Seth's, spoken with his dry, dry inflection.

She covered her mouth instantly, her eyes widening, and watched Raymond, certain his fury would be absolute.

Instead, he laughed. It burst out of him and he pressed his mouth into the crook of his arm to smother it. He shook with laughter. Taking short steps, he moved over to the rocking chair and sank into it, still wracked with tremors.

Natasha watched him, completely flummoxed. How could he find such outright defiance amusing?

Finally, he sat back with a sigh, one boot thrust out to stop himself from rocking violently on the chair. He looked up at the ceiling and gave out a gusty exhalation. Then he thrust himself to his feet once more and came over to her so he could speak quietly.

He rested his hand against hers where it gripped the

bedpost and bent toward her. "It could have been Seth standing there, indignant and furious. I heard him say that many times, only never in polite company." He smiled. "You even had the accent exactly right." He waved his other hand, to take in her clothes. "Looking as you do, it was twice the surprise, yet you were perfectly correct to refuse me. I have no right to demand anything of you. You have earned your independence and I will abide by it."

"Oh." She suddenly felt light. Airy.

"I would only ask that you be especially wary when you are in the company of this Morven Fortescue. She hides more than she reveals, as her conversations with you in the past have hinted."

"You will not tell me why you dislike her?"

"I do not dislike her," Raymond said, surprising her. "I simply do not trust her, now I have seen her, for reasons I cannot explain right now."

"I will be wary, then," Natasha told him. She hesitated. "Actually, I do not like her very much. I had decided that I would not speak to her again, even before I abandoned her in the park."

He considered her. "Yet you grew angry when I suggested the same."

"You were telling me what to do," she said. "I did not like it."

"I can see that a life with you in it would be a challenging one," he murmured.

Her heart squeezed. She stared at him, wondering if she had misheard.

Raymond kissed her. It was a raw, ragged press of his mouth against hers. It was as if he was trying to say something with his lips that he would not say aloud. There was a fervor in it that she had not felt in any of his previous seventeen kisses. Her grip on the bedpost was loosened as he drew her to him. His hand plunged into her hair, scattering more loosened clips onto the floor. She was pulled up onto her toes, his arm around her back keeping her upright.

Natasha moaned into his mouth. There was a recklessness to his kiss that shot her pulse into the sky. The weakening wave of longing was hotter. Wilder.

When his hand cupped her breasts through the jacket of her morning suit, she barely held back her cry of pleasure. The intense spike of lust seemed to arrow straight to her mound.

Yet it still wasn't enough. Natasha stepped away from him and unbuttoned the jacket with trembling hands as Raymond watched her with hooded eyes. When the jacket was open, she picked up his hand and slid it inside, over her corset and camisole, so his fingertips brushed the mound of her breast. Her trembling intensified.

Raymond's exhalation was as unsteady as hers.

Natasha reached for the fastening on her skirt. He gripped her arm and held her still. "Wait," he said softly.

"Why?" she asked bluntly.

He closed her jacket and fastened one of the buttons so it would stay closed, then put his hands around her waist. His thumbs moved in restlessly little circles against her stomach. "You have claimed the right to make your own decisions and so you shall." He brushed her hair back over her shoulder and she thought she could detect a fine trembling in his hand. "I am an interloper here today. When you invite me back into this room, I will know you are driven by more than the power of my kiss, that you have made a choice."

Chapter Eleven

The new rail line from Falmouth to Truro made travelling by train to Innesford House far more convenient. However, as Natasha had left everyone behind in London to pack and follow her to Cornwall, there was no one at the house to meet her train. The house would still be closed up for summer as Natasha had sent no word on when she was to arrive.

Normally, a family who lived in one of the cottages tucked in around the cathedral prepared Innesford House for the end of the London season, when the family returned for the start of the hunting season and winter.

Natasha left her trunk and bags with the station porter, then walked from the new train station, which still smelled of paint and tar, to the Smith cottage. The walk was not taxing, for all her strenuous walking in Hyde Park over the last few weeks had improved her wind. She enjoyed the warm day, for while it was nearly September, summer still held its grip.

Harry Smith, the father, was startled but civil and roused his children with a great shout up the stairs, bringing them tumbling down in a hurry to fetch the cart, hitch the horse and gather supplies.

Mrs. Smith put together a basket of sandwiches and a flask of tea, for Natasha's supper. Natasha sat up the front of the cart, on the hard wooden seat beside Mr. Smith, with the supper basket between them. The three nearly grown girls and his oldest son Brian, who was already a man, sat in the back with the buckets and rags and Mr. Smith's big box of tools.

Mr. Smith pulled the cart up to the front of the house. Natasha unlocked the door and stepped inside. The rooms didn't quite echo as she walked through them, although they did feel empty.

Unlike many of the big country houses belonging to upper class families, Innesford House was shut down each March, when the family moved to London for the Season. Natasha could not bear the idea of leaving her children in the country for nearly half the year while she galivanted around London. Seth had been apoplectic at the idea when he had first realized what was expected of them if they were to maintain their social standing. "We'll take the bloody household with us," he muttered. "They can hold their balls and their regattas and we'll hold our family together, too." Seth had gotten his way, even though it was one more ripple of notoriety among the *ton* for their family and their peculiarities.

The stigma faded somewhat the next year, when Elisa and Vaughn had brought their children with them to London, too, and leased one of the largest houses in St. James to accommodate them. Rhys and Annalies never left London except to travel to Cornwall for the Great Family Gathering. Their house was a roomy Georgian mansion at the northern end of Hyde Park, large enough to accommodate all seven of their adopted and natural off-spring.

Mr. Smith and his son moved off around the outside of the house to check shutters and windows to see how they had fared over summer, for some of the storms that raged across the Cornish coast were severe. For generations, ships had foundered on Cornish cliffs during storms, some of them deliberately enticed there by wreckers who would plunder the helpless ships for valuables.

While Mr. Smith inspected the gardens and the outside of the house, Natasha moved through the silent rooms. Everything was covered in white cloths, giving the rooms a ghostly, insubstantial feel. Natasha asked the girls to open the big doors onto the back terrace and some of the front windows, to encourage a cross-breeze, for it was musty and still.

Then she climbed the stairs to the first floor. There were three floors altogether, including the ground floor and not counting the attic floor where the servants were quartered. The main bedroom suites and guest rooms were on the first floor. The children's dormitories were on the second floor.

At the end of the wide passage on the first floor was the master suite, proclaimed by the twin doors with their gilt flourishes and white paint.

Natasha opened the door and looked inside. The dresser by the window was wearing a white sheet. The massive four-poster bed with its Corinthian columns and curved canopy was too large for any yardage to cover. The mattress had been draped with a simple cover, one that could be washed.

She had spent twenty years sleeping beside Seth in that

bed. She had given birth to seven children here, too. The houses in London had changed over the years, but not this one. Even Harrow Hall in Ireland did not have the connection to Seth that this room did.

Natasha gripped the door handle, until the filigree dug into her palm. Then, softly and slowly, she closed the door once more.

Moving down the passage, crossing from side to side, she opened every bedroom door to look inside. Some of the rooms were spoken for. Cian and Neil and even Lilly had their rooms on this floor. They had graduated to the first floor from the dormitories when Natasha had considered them mature enough for their own rooms. This year, she would give one of the rooms to Daniel, too. He was fifteen and ready to become a man.

Then there were the two suites that Annalies and Rhys, Elisa and Vaughn used when they stayed here. The remaining bedrooms were used by adult guests, including Elisa and Anna's grown children. Natasha did not manage their assignments. Corcoran took care of that headache.

At the far end of the passage, there was another small suite that was the last to be used for accommodations, because it had odd angles and strange nooks and crannies that made it difficult to fit useful furniture anywhere along the walls. Yet it had a view of the ocean and the southern sun played on the walls. Ivy grew up the outer wall and framed the windows.

Natasha stepped inside, looking around. The bed was another antique, only the slender posts were white and it didn't have a canopy. The walls of the room had also been painted white, which made the room bright and cheerful.

There were three doors on the wall facing the bed. Two of them were storage rooms that could be used as wardrobes. The third door, the one closest to the window, had a lock and key. She turned the key and opened the door to reveal a narrow corridor. She passed through the corridor to an adjoining bedroom that was just as small and charming as the first.

Natasha ran her hand over the carved footboard of the bed and looked out the west-facing window, down onto the orchard and pottager garden below. To the far left was the sea and the headland. Gulls circled over the headland, their white bodies almost shining in the afternoon sunlight. It was a highly domestic scene, that guests would consider inferior to the better view of the sea available in the other rooms. She liked it, though.

Pleased, Natasha went out to the main passage once more and looked to her left. The door to the second bedroom was opposite this room's door. Anyone who was not intimate with the layout of the house might not suspect they were connected.

Polly, the oldest of Mr. Smith's girls, climbed to the top of the stairs and looked around. "We've opened up the house, my lady. Should we take all the sheets and cloths off?"

"No. Leave them for now." Natasha indicated the room behind her. "I would like this suite dusted and cleaned and the bed made. Also, the adjoining room. That is all I need for now. The permanent staff will be here in a day or two and the whole house can be cleaned then. It is too large a task for just the three of you."

"Yes, my lady." Polly dashed downstairs again, her boots clattering on the stairs.

Natasha followed her down more slowly and went to find Mr. Smith to ask that he take her back to the train station to pick up her trunk and baggage. She glanced at the blue face of the ormolu clock on the buffet in the drawing room.

As coincidence would have it, she would arrive at the station around the same time as the four o'clock train.

* * * * *

Natasha was checking to ensure the last of the baggage was squeezed onto Mr. Smith's cart when the train clanked and hissed to a stop by the platform.

Mr. Smith scratched his head as he looked at the pile in the little cart. "Perhaps we could leave one or two of them behind and arrange for them to be delivered later, my lady," he suggested.

"Why don't you go ahead with all of them?" Natasha replied. "I will find one of the local hackneys and follow. When you have delivered the trunks, you and your family should go home for supper. Thanks to your wife's sandwiches, I will be quite content by myself for the evening."

"As you will, my lady. A plank is no seat for a gentle-woman, anyway." He climbed up onto the bench, picked up the reins and clicked his tongue to get the pony moving. It plodded off, the wheels of the cart groaning under the weight of the trunks.

Natasha turned to survey the platform. The train would not return to London, for this was the last run for the day. It hissed steadily.

There were few passengers left, who were clearly waiting for rides. One of them was tall, dark haired and broad-shouldered. He was holding a single bag.

Natasha went up to him. "Lord Marblethorpe."

He turned, his gaze moving from her hems to her hair. Heat flickered in his eyes, then vanished. "Lady Innesford," he said formally, for there were others nearby.

"I was about to hire a hackney to return to the house. Would you care to share my ride?"

"I have a room at the Rising Sun. I don't want to take you out of your way."

"It is only a little out of the way and I would like to hear how your mother fares."

"Very well then." He stepped aside and she moved past him and down the steps to the station road. There were two hacks standing by, anticipating possible fares. She moved up to the first. Raymond flipped a coin to the driver and passed up his bag. Then he opened the door for her.

"Please tell him to take us directly to Innesford House," she told Raymond and climbed into the coach.

She heard Raymond murmur to the driver, then he stepped up inside and shut the door. He settled on the oppo-site seat and rested his gloved hands on his knees. His dark gaze met hers. "Well, I am here, as requested."

"Yes."

"The house, Natasha?" he asked softly. "Isn't it still closed up?"

"Yes." She looked back at him steadily and saw his chest rise as he drew in a deep breath and let it out.

"There are sandwiches and whatever we can scavenge from Cook's pantry," she continued. "I imagine there is brandy in the library, too, although it won't be in a decanter."

"Bottles pour as readily as decanters." He shrugged. "Can you manage without a maid? How long until Corcoran and the staff return?"

"Corcoran will be here tomorrow afternoon, along with the rest of the staff." She kept her gaze on his face. "You will have to help me with my things."

His eyes narrowed into the sleepy, heated expression she had seen most often just after he had kissed her. Her heart leapt.

"Natasha…" He leaned forward.

"No." She shook her head and looked up at the roof of the coach, to where the driver would be sitting. If they spoke quietly enough, the driver could not hear them over the clack of the horse's shoes on the cobbles and the jingle of the harness, A sudden shift of weight inside the coach *would* be noticed.

He sat back with a tiny hiss of frustration and looked out the window at the rows of cottages as they passed by. His hand curled into a fist on his knee and stayed there.

It was a silent journey back to the house, which lay five

miles beyond Truro. As the miles rolled on, Natasha's heart beat faster and faster. Even though she had laid awake at night planning out this day and thought she had weighed up the risks, she still trembled at her own daring.

Then she would look at Raymond. He watched her without cease, his eyes narrowed speculatively. Her heart and her belly would flutter. She would gauge the width of his shoulders under the jacket and imagine what lay beneath and her whole body would throb.

It took forever to reach the house.

Raymond handed her out of the carriage. Mr. Smith's cart had gone. Natasha unlocked the house with the old iron key and held the door open. "Come in," she told Raymond.

He took off his hat. "This seems very strange," he murmured. "I don't think I have seen this house anything other than completely stuffed full of people."

Natasha's trunks and baggage were sitting on the front hall tiles. Raymond gave them a startled glance, then dropped his own bag next to them. He walked through the hall into the big drawing room on the other side of the arch, with its magnificent view of the sea.

Natasha took the two steps up to the drawing room. "We are completely alone here," she told him.

Raymond met her eyes.

Natasha picked up her skirt once more. "I'll show you where your room is."

He glanced out through the big French doors.

Natasha knew what he was thinking. "The carriage house is not for you anymore," she told him.

He considered her. "Then perhaps you had better show me the way. It has been so long since I was upstairs here, I cannot recall where everything is."

They climbed up the stairs, Raymond keeping pace with her. At the top, he glanced to the left, along the corridor toward the white and gold doors. Natasha turned to the right and moved down the passage to the doors at the other end. She pointed to the one on the right. "This will be your room while you are here."

Raymond reached for the door.

Natasha turned away and crossed the hall runner to the other door and opened it. She turned back to face Raymond. "This is my room," she added.

Raymond didn't move. She knew he was waiting for her, waiting for a sign.

She held out her hand.

It had been her intention to take his hand and draw him into her room, only Raymond did not give her the opportunity to do that. He gripped her hand and pulled her up against him, his strong arm around her back. Her feet left the floor as his lips met hers. He carried her into the room. The door slammed behind him.

Natasha ceased to care about externalities after that. Raymond was kissing her and she did not have to worry about who might see, who might hear, none of it. She could just enjoy his kiss and how it made her feel.

He put her back on the floor but didn't move away from her. Instead, he brushed a loose curl from her forehead then held her face in both hands. His gaze roved over her, as if he was memorizing the image.

Then, with a groan, he kissed her again.

Natasha could tell that Raymond had removed the brakes on his control. He was driving forward with all the pent up energy from weeks of kisses and careful circling. Now, all that was behind him.

It felt as though he was trying to consume her. His arms were vises, crushing her to him.

Natasha didn't mind. If he had not been holding her, she wasn't sure she would be able to stand properly. Her legs were trembling. All of her was shaking. For her, too, the brakes were off. There was only one end to this moment and she ached to reach it.

With Raymond's mouth on hers, his tongue teasing her lips and teeth, she reached up and pushed his coat off his shoulders. It fell with a muffled thump to the ground. Then the cravat. She worked it loose and threw it behind her. Her fingers felt clumsy and thick as she tried to undo the buttons on his waistcoat.

He finally broke the kiss. "Let me," he said. He worked the buttons swiftly, easing them undone, then shrugged out of the waistcoat. The shirt billowed around his waist and the weight of the collar pulled the opening apart, revealing his strong neck and a glimpse of his chest. There was no undershirt beneath and her heart thudded unevenly.

Raymond turned away, pulling the cufflinks from the cuffs and dropping them on the window sill. Then, while still standing at the window, he pulled the shirt over his head and dropped it on the chair in the corner.

His back was as broad as Natasha had suspected it to be. It arrowed down to a tight waist, under the trousers. His rear…it was high and hard beneath the wool. She swallowed.

He turned to face her. Natasha took a breath as her gaze skittered over his chest. The low rise of the muscle at the top, the two flat brown nipples, which were as hard and tight as her own. His stomach wasn't flat as she had thought a fit man's stomach would be. It was ridged by muscles beneath the flesh, that moved as he did, making his stomach ripple… Natasha swallowed. The power and vitality those ridges implied made her heart flutter.

She couldn't help but drop her gaze down lower. The front of his trousers was tented, the fabric strained.

Her heart leapt, ramming itself against her chest. Lust curled at the bottom of her belly, making her aware of the saddle of flesh between her legs.

The reality of Raymond was far better than anything she had imagined. She had not suspected a man could look so… primal.

He lifted a hand and pointed to her head. "Let down your hair for me." His voice was harsh. Stressed.

Natasha had fixed her hair earlier in the afternoon, on the train. She had learned from Annalies how to coil her hair on the back of her head in a way that required only two clips to hold it. She removed the clips now and shook her hair, letting the weight of her hair fall down her back.

Raymond drew in a heavy, startled breath. His eyes closed. Then he opened them again.

"What is wrong?" she asked, alarmed.

"Not a thing," he said. "In my imagination, I have seen you do that many times." He smiled. "With your hair down, you look barely sixteen and ripe for plucking."

Natasha smiled, feeling a sense of wickedness slide over her. "I am not sixteen. I know far more than any sixteen-year-old girl possibly could and all of it will benefit you."

His jaw rippled. "Your jacket. Take it off."

She lifted her hands to the buttons. The overwhelming rush of pleasure had subsided a little and now she could manipulate the buttons quickly, as it was something she did every day. The jacket fell open, the heavy embellishments pulling it aside, revealing her corset cover and the top edge of her camisole.

For a moment, she hesitated. She had never been undressed in front of any man but Seth. Only, the heated look in Raymond's eyes encouraged her to continue. She would do anything to keep that look in his eyes. It was making her feel weak and feminine and desired.

She pulled the jacket off and handed it to him. Raymond dropped it onto the chair next to him without looking. His gaze stayed on her.

Natasha continued. She unbuttoned the camisole cover and gave him that, too. If anything, the heat and lust in his eyes intensified and she realized that disrobing in this way was arousing him. He was enjoying watching her take off her clothes.

She reached behind her and unbuttoned the skirt. The gabardine loosened around her waist, but did not fall because the hoops and petticoats were holding it up. She tugged at the drawstrings and the bow unraveled. The petticoat and hoop dropped to the floor about her feet, the skirt on top of them.

That left her in her corset and camisole, pantalets, stockings and shoes.

Raymond drew in a breath. She could see he was fighting to stay still. There was a pulse beating at the base of his powerful neck, telling her he was not nearly as calm as he appeared.

Natasha eased the hooks undone on the front of the corset, moving with practiced speed. She took it off and handed it over to Raymond, the stays hanging from it.

He tossed it on to the chair. "The camisole buttons," he said and his voice was so strained she barely recognized it.

She raised her hands to the center of the camisole. Now her corset was removed, the camisole was loose around her torso and the cotton rubbed against the sensitive tips of her breasts. The brush of the fabric was maddening. She ached for Raymond to touch them without the layer of camisole in the way.

She untied the ribbon and slipped the tiny pearl buttons undone, moving down from the top.

Raymond swallowed. She could see his throat work.

She paused, with half the buttons loosened. "My turn," she declared.

He groaned. "No, I beg you. Continue."

She shook her head and stepped over the mound of skirt and petticoats and hoops, bent and swept them up, then carried them over to the chair and dumped them. She turned to

Raymond. "Come here."

He took the small pace needed to bring him before her. The stiff congestion at the front of his trousers looked even more pronounced.

Natasha could barely breathe with excitement. She eased the top button undone, then the next. Then a thought struck her and a little thrill of excitement speared her, making her nub throb with the promise of her idea. "You do it," she told Raymond. "I want to watch."

"God help me," he breathed. "This is torment." He lifted his hands to the buttons and unfastened three of them, quickly. Then the next. The fabric separated and she could see soft flesh behind. Dark hair arrowed downwards. Natasha had not realized how exciting it was to glimpse something as simple as a man's body hair in this way.

He undid another button.

Natasha licked her lips, wondering when the rest of him would appear and eager to see it.

He groaned. "No. Enough," he said, his voice ragged. He picked her up, startling her. His hands came under her bottom and he pulled her against him, forcing her knees to part around his hips. She could feel his thick, rigid shaft against the very center of her and a moan slipped from her lips. Dear God in heaven, he was hot and hard and felt wonderful against her. What would it feel like when his trousers were not in the way and her pantalets were gone? Except they were split in the center and with just a bit of wriggling, she could perhaps separate the edges…

Raymond kissed her. There was nothing gentle about this

kiss. His tongue thrust into her mouth, almost as if he were claiming her. The urgency, the wildness of his kiss sent flames washing through her, setting fire to every nerve she possessed. She heard herself make the same raw sound.

She felt a wall against her back.

Raymond tore his mouth from hers. He was breathing heavily, almost panting, his chest rising and falling rapidly. He fumbled, his hand brushing her bottom. Then her pantalets were drawn apart, exposing her.

Natasha caught her breath in a gasp as she realized what Raymond intended to do. It was too late. His hands came back under her, holding her up. She felt the head of his shaft up against her. She was slick with moisture and more than ready and he slid inside her in one hard, deep thrust and grew still.

His breath pushed out in a ragged gust. His eyes held hers as they paused, both panting.

The overwhelming sensation was one of heat and thickness. He was large inside her and the flesh around him rippled with delight. She could feel herself squeezing him. It was so very, very good!

Natasha put her hands on his shoulders. She felt the heat of his flesh and the softness of it. Beneath the softness was iron muscle and bone, and tendons that flexed as he supported her.

"More," she whispered.

"Jesus wept," he breathed. One hand let her go and reached up quickly to her camisole. He gripped it and tore it apart, exposing her torso and her breasts. He bent his head and took a nipple in his mouth.

Natasha cried out. The so very sensitive tip was nipped and teased by his tongue and teeth. The tugging was gloriously delicious. His tongue rasped over the very end, sending a shooting spark of pleasure bolting through her, directly to her nub, that gave out a heavy throb. She made a sound that was guttural and alien to her ears. She had never made a sound like that before.

Her channel squeezed and gripped him in response. She felt him jerk inside her. A strained note came from his throat and his hips flexed. His shaft shifted and thrust back into her. The movement pushed her nub against him and her pleasure built higher.

"More," she begged. "Please don't stop."

He worked his body against her and inside her. With a gasp, he lifted his head from her breast. The tendons in his throat flexed as he moved. He looked like a man driven to the very brink of some madness.

Her climbing pleasure stole her attention. It felt as if her entire body gathered around his shaft and focused there. She shook, almost frightened by the awful power of the coming peak.

It burst over her, stealing her breath and her thoughts. Her heart seemed to stop. For an endless moment she hung suspended in a sea of pure sensation, so bright and fiery she could see and hear nothing.

Raymond gave a choked cry, smothering it against her flesh. He jerked inside her and grew still, all except his breath, which came in ragged sips.

Her own breath was no steadier. That was the only sound in the room, the two of them breathing.

Raymond reached up and curled his hand behind her neck and drew her face down so he could kiss her. Then he eased her off the wall and carried her over to the bed.

She had failed to notice what bedclothes the girls had put on the bed. It felt like satin beneath her shoulders.

Raymond slipped out of her and for the first time she saw the red, pulsing length of him. It glistened from her moisture.

He bent and stripped his boots and trousers and underwear away in three quick movements. When he straightened again, he was completely naked. His shaft jutted from his thighs as he looked down at her with his hooded eyes.

Her channel clenched in reaction. She wanted him back in her.

Wordlessly, he stripped her of her sopping pantalets and the ruined camisole. He left her stockings and shoes in place and pulled her toward him. He was going to take her again right now, this instant. It was exactly what she wanted and she sighed as he gripped her hips with his big hands and slid back into her.

He did not only take his pleasure. His thumbs moved restlessly over the indentations next to her hip bones, making her flesh quiver with the exquisite thrill of his touch. Then he reached farther over and down, sliding one thumb up against her nub.

She gasped with delight. With his hips thrusting against her, he barely had to move his thumb. It nudged the proud flesh, making her writhe and groan as the pleasure leapt to life again, turning her into a mindless, greedy vessel.

Her pleasure peaked twice before Raymond finished and on the second occasion, her groan was so loud and harsh it was almost a scream. Raymond flexed and slammed into her, in rapid, hard little thrusts, his eyes closing. Then, with a harsh cry of his own, he spent himself.

He bent over the bed, propping himself up on one arm, as he recovered. Then he let her go and climbed onto the bed next to her.

"You don't want to get *in* the bed?" she asked.

He turned her on her side, so her bottom was against him and kissed her cheek, as he brought his arm over her waist. He cupped her breast, his thumb stroking the nipple, which grew sharp and sensitive almost at once.

"Why would I want to get into bed?" he breathed against her neck and slid his tongue over her flesh, making her shiver.

The stroking of her breast, the feel of his still firm shaft against her bottom and his hot breath against her, left Natasha unable to keep still. She writhed, little thrills spilling through her.

After a while, he lifted her knee over his. As he slid into her once more, this time from behind, Natasha realized that Raymond was an untapped, depthless well of passion. He had only just begun. She had unleashed an overwhelming force.

She trembled with pleasure at the thought.

Chapter Twelve

"Do you have any idea what the time might be?" Natasha asked, turning her head on the pillow so she may look at Raymond.

He let the locks of her hair drop from his fingers in a cascade, so they rained upon her back. She lay on her stomach and wore no clothes. The bedsheets were kicked down the end of the bed where they had stayed for hours now. It was morning, although she was not certain about how late in the morning it was. She'd had very little sleep during the night. Nevertheless, she felt wonderful—alive in a way she could not remember since she was much younger.

Raymond lay on his side, his head propped on his arm, facing her. Even when he was resting, he could not seem to stop trailing his fingertips over her flesh, or playing with her hair, as he was now.

He let his hand drop and looked at her. There was a peacefulness in his eyes she had never seen before. It was as if the shield he held up to everyone else had gone and she was seeing his true nature.

"I imagine it must be somewhere around nine in the morning," he said. "My watch stopped just after three this morning. Why? Are you hungry?"

"The sandwiches are all gone, so it doesn't really matter whether I am hungry or not." She stretched and rolled on to her side, facing him. "We should take advantage of the day to ourselves. The children and the staff will arrive later."

He picked up her hand, curled her fingers over his and raised it to his mouth and kissed the back of it. His lips were warm. "And then what happens?"

Her heart gave a little leap. "I rather hope Cook brings a pot of something or other with her from London. I am sure we'll all be starving by then."

Raymond shook his head. "You know very well what I am asking. Do you misinterpret me to give yourself time to answer, or to avoid answering altogether?"

Natasha dropped her gaze to the sheet between them. "Both," she admitted.

"Ah." He lifted her chin. His gaze was steady. "If I were any other man, I would insist that we be married as swiftly as possible, after yesterday and this morning. I think you know that. The only reason I do not, is because you have earned the right to make such decisions for yourself."

"You do not feel unmanned by my independence?"

Raymond smiled. "If I were not a man, I would not be here and you would not be looking as you do this morning. You know I am man enough. I have no need to demonstrate the fact to the rest of the world by forcing you to the altar."

Her heart picked up even more speed. "Please do not ask me," she said softly. "I need time, Raymond. This…" She spread her hand over the sheet. "It will sound awful, but I needed to put this out of the way, first. Now, at last, I believe I may be able to think a little more clearly. Can you do that? Can you give me time?"

"Can you give me the nights?" he asked. He glanced at the interconnecting door that led to his room. "I believe that was your intention all along."

"Is it very wicked of me to ask for only this, for now?" She could feel her cheeks burning. "Marriage *would* remove the sin, only it is not just me I must think about. There are my children—lord, Raymond, there is your son to think of, too. Our families, the Great Family. I haven't even thought what the *ton* may think of us—"

"Shh…" He said it softly. "We cannot rush any decision. I agree. It must be thought through very carefully. In the meantime, we will keep this for us alone." He pressed his hand over hers on the sheet.

"You must think things through, too, Raymond," she said gently.

"I?"

She drew in a breath for courage, then spoke the words. "I would not have you marry me simply because I allowed you this privilege." She shifted her hand on the sheet. "I am not a virtuous maid whose reputation must be preserved. I am a woman of means. I would not have you feel obligated because of my wanton ways."

Raymond grew very still. He watched her as if he were a hawk and she were prey.

"Then, there is Susanna," Natasha added softly, knowing it must be said.

He sat up abruptly and curled his arms about his knees and stared at the foot of the bed. "We agreed that Seth and Susanna were behind us."

"Seth *is* in my past," Natasha said gently. "Susanna still moves among us, yes?"

"You would not allow that I may have learned how to let her go?" he asked quietly.

"Have you?" she asked, genuinely curious.

"You do not know that answer for yourself?"

"How could I? You will not speak of her. You say it would compromise her to do so, yet that conveniently means I will never learn about her. You know so much about Seth and I know nothing of the woman who took your heart, not even if you still love her."

"Does that matter?" he asked, his voice low. "Marriages are made for other reasons besides love, as much as the *ton* would like to pretend otherwise." He spoke bitterly and she remembered the pressure his father's family had put upon him to marry Rose.

"I married for love," Natasha said simply. "I cannot fathom ever marrying for anything else."

His shoulders were held stiff and straight. He was still looking away from her, refusing to meet her gaze. "I see," he said softly. Then, astonishingly, he laughed. It was not a humorous sound. It was strained.

Then Natasha's stomach growled loudly.

Raymond immediately turned to her, his face concerned, as she sat up, her hand to her stomach. "You *are* hungry! You should have said so."

"I didn't think I was. What are you doing?"

For Raymond had risen and was thrusting his legs into his trousers.

"I think I spotted a fruitcake at the back of the pantry, where I found the matches, last night." For they had not been able to light a candle without matches and neither of them had such an item in their possession.

"If there is a cake in the pantry, it would be months old by now," Natasha said doubtfully.

"Does your cook use lots of brandy?" Raymond asked.

"Oh, yes," she said, with a smile.

"Then it may still be good, especially if she wrapped it properly. I'll see what else is down there, as well. There may well be some jam we could put on the cake."

Natasha wrinkled her nose. Her stomach rumbled again. That decided her. She got to her feet and picked up the wrapper that Raymond had retrieved from her trunks for her, on the same match-hunting expedition. "I will come with you. It would be easier to eat in the kitchen, anyway."

Raymond opened the bedroom door and Natasha hurried after him. She nearly cannoned into him when he came to a sharp stop in the middle of the hall runner. She steadied herself against him, her hands on his bare back.

"Cian!" Raymond said sharply.

Natasha looked around, startled.

Her oldest son stood at the top of the stairs, his hand on the newel post, one foot on the carpet. He had frozen in the act of taking the very last step up into the corridor. His blue eyes, so like his father's, were wide, as he looked from Raymond to Natasha.

His face blanched.

"Cian," Natasha said quickly, holding out her hand and

coming toward him. "We should sit down and talk. I didn't expect you home so early…"

"Clearly," Cian said. His tone was dry. He turned and hurried down the stairs again.

"No, Cian! Please!" Natasha called out to him. She hurried over to the railing at the top of the stairwell and leaned over it, watching him descend, his long legs moving swiftly. "At least give me a chance to explain," she begged him.

He looked up at her as he turned at the landing. He paused long enough to say: "Nothing needs explaining. It is all perfectly clear, Mother." He hurried down the stairs and out of sight.

Natasha gripped the varnished wood railing, the sick feeling in her belly and her chest making her heart work unpleasantly.

She hurried back to the bedroom, for Raymond was no longer standing in the middle of the corridor. He was, instead, dressing faster than she thought it was possible for a man to dress. He was tucking in his shirt and fastening his trousers as she entered. He already wore his boots. As the collar and cuffs were still pinned to his shirt, all he needed to do was tie the cravat and fasten his waistcoat.

"What are you doing?" Natasha breathed.

"Going after him," Raymond said flatly.

Natasha wrung her hands together. "Is that wise? Are you not the focus of his…ill feelings?"

Raymond flung on his coat, picked up the cravat and stuffed it in his pocket. He had not bothered with the waistcoat. He came over to her, moving fast, and kissed her cheek. "As much as you may not appreciate hearing this, I must point out that right now, *you* are the focus of his bad graces. Trust me. I know what he is feeling. Let me deal with it."

Before she could argue or protest, he was gone. She heard his boots on the runner beyond the door, then the clatter of them on the stairs.

* * * * *

When Raymond didn't find Cian anywhere on the estate, he saddled a horse and rode into Truro. There were not many places in Truro where an angry young man would attempt to go to ground. Cian was in the first location Raymond tried. Raymond moved through the nearly empty inn to the bench in the back of the room, under the high window. Cian had already emptied a full tankard of ale. He was working on the second as Raymond settled on the stool opposite him.

Cian scowled. "I should beat your face bloody."

"Do you think that would help?" Raymond asked him curiously. "You can try, if you believe it will."

"Try?" Cian snorted and drank deeply again. "I grew up with you whaling the tar out of me every time I looked sideways. I believe I have already been suitably embarrassed today."

"Your mother did not intend to embarrass you."

Cian scowled at him. "If I had not returned from Cambridge early and found out for myself, how many others would be laughing behind my back about my immoral mother?"

Raymond leaned forward. "Hear me, Cian. Hear me well. I know you are angry and you have some justification for that, which is why I am here. However, if you refer to your mother again in terms other than those of utmost respect, then I *will* take you outside and whale the tar out of you."

Cian blinked. His blue eyes were identical to Seth's. The high cheekbones were Natasha's. His height and his angularity were all his own. "How long?" he asked, his voice strained.

Raymond knew what he was asking in his growing inebriation. "Those within the family who spent the summer in London are aware that your mother and I have become friends. That is the extent of their awareness. Beyond the family, all appears as it should be."

"And what I saw, back at the house?"

"That is between your mother and I," Raymond told him.

Cian scowled at him. "Are you going to marry her?"

Raymond drew in a breath and let it out, giving himself time to think. "Does Tommy Winston still call you Blue-Boy?" he asked. In Cian's first year at Eton, the Winston boy had thought it the height of amusement to mispronounce Cian's name, deliberately. Instead of "kee-an", Tommy and his cronies had called Cian "cyan", which had quickly become "blue-boy".

"What has that to do with—"

"Bear with me. Tommy and his friends are all at Cambridge, too, aren't they? Do they still bother you?"

"Not since I grew taller than everyone," Cian replied, his tone dark.

Raymond didn't pursue the inference. He remembered his college days all too well. The pecking order wasn't always based on rank. Sometimes, upper body strength and good footwork made the difference. If Cian had inherited his father's love of a scrap, then Tommy Winston and his obnoxious friends would have learned the hard way how to pronounce Cian's name properly.

"Do you remember when you came home at the end of the first term at Eton," Raymond said, "and your mother found out what Winston and his friends were doing to you?" The teasing had not stopped at name-calling. There had been crueler pranks.

Cian grinned at the memory. "I thought she might explode."

Raymond nodded. "I think even your father had trouble preventing her from travelling to the Winston estate in Sussex and taking it up with Tommy's parents."

Cian's smile grew warmer, his gaze distant, as he remembered the moment. "Mother was beside herself…" His smile faded as he refocused on Raymond. "What of it?"

"Your mother is a strong woman, Cian. She had to be, with Seth gone so often on his voyages to Australia and she had to be strong to match Seth, too. She has borne seven children, runs two estates and maintains an impeccable reputation so that you and your brothers and sisters will have a place in society when you come of age."

"I *am* of age," Cian pointed out.

"And you are reaping the benefits of everything your mother has done for you. Your inheritance is intact and in better standing than ever before. Your mother did all that." Raymond sat back. "Do you believe for a second that a woman who knows her own mind as your mother does would not insist upon self-determination?"

Cian squeezed the skin over the bridge of his nose with his long fingers. "You asked her and she said no?"

"I have failed to ask her because I *know* the answer would be no...for now."

"Then you have honorable intentions?"

Raymond smiled. "My intentions have always been honorable. A woman like your mother, though, does not buckle for just any man. It has been an interesting summer."

Cian frowned. "I am trying to encompass this. You grew up with us, Raymond. You were one of us. Now you are... what, exactly?"

"I am still your cousin by name," Raymond said gently. "I always will be. Now, though, the shape of the family is shifting a little."

"Or a lot, if you have your way," Cian said, scowling harder.

"That is not a given. Not yet." Raymond lifted his hand at the innkeeper and held up two fingers. The innkeeper bowed and scurried off for another two tankards. "Would you share a drink with me, Cian?"

Cian considered him. "Are you staying at the house?"

"Your mother wishes me to."

His scowl deepened. "Are we to be subjected to more of that display I saw earlier?"

"That was unfortunate," Raymond admitted. "Because of the ill-timing, I will indulge your question this one time. In the future, I would consider such a question to be impertinent and disrespectful toward your mother. Are we clear?"

Cian considered him for a moment. Quietly, he said, "Clear." Then he drank heavily once more.

"Then I will answer the question. There will be no display, no hint of impropriety, nothing that would arouse even mild suspicion. Your mother will be as devoted to you and your brothers and sisters as she has always been. Nothing will change, except that I will be a guest. In public, the entire family will be models of deportment and do nothing to tarnish the family's good name...no matter what they may come to suspect of private matters inside the family."

"Inside the family..." Cian muttered.

"...we do as we please," Raymond finished.

Cian sat up. "I will drink with you," he declared, as the innkeeper placed the fresh tankards on the table and swept up the old ones.

Raymond relaxed. He took a mouthful of the ale and wiped the froth away. "How is it you are home so early, anyway?" he demanded. "Did you run away?"

"I was given leave. I wanted to discuss something with Mother..." Cian's scowl came back in a rush. "The Queen is to issue the last list of honors for the Crimea War next month."

"I had heard," Raymond said.

Cian gulped the fresh brew as if he was drawing courage from it. He put the tankard down a little unsteadily. "My father is not on the list. *Again*."

"Seth fought in the Crimea War?" Raymond asked, amazed. "I do not remember that," he added carefully.

Cian leaned forward and lowered his voice. "He did not go to Russia. He did something here in England. Agents and all the clandestine business that happens far behind the front lines. You know." Cian gripped his tankard, his knuckles white. "He died for Queen and country. He should be honored for it."

Raymond stared at Cian, his thoughts racing. "I heard that Seth died of blackwater fever, that he brought back with him from Australia."

Cian snorted. "There is no blackwater fever in Australia." He leaned even closer. "It is all part of the secrecy, yes?"

"Who told you your father was an agent for the Queen?" Raymond asked, keeping his tone light, even though his heart was squeezing.

"Mother, of course. Oh, she was never blunt about it. The hints were enough for me to put it all together. That is why I wanted to discuss it with her. The insult to my father's memory can't be allowed to slide."

Raymond shook his head. "You may be stirring things up that should be left alone, Cian. The stealthy affairs of that type are often tied up with heads of state. To acknowledge your father's role in them openly, as war honors would do, may jeopardize the stability of Europe. Do you see that no insult is intended?"

It was pure bluff. Raymond fervently hoped that Cian's grasp of politics and furtive military affairs was weak enough that he would accept Raymond's theory. That way, the man—who was still a boy in many ways—could find a way to live with himself and with Seth's death.

It also would prevent Cian from asking the question that Raymond now held in his heart.

How did Seth Williams really die?

Chapter Thirteen

When the girls were finally asleep in their gently rocking berths, Lilly carefully slid the compartment door closed and made her way to the lounge area at the front of the carriage. The entire Wardell family was travelling to Kirkaldy for the winter instead of Farleigh Hall, because both Will and Vaughn hated the hall. The longer journey required they travel by sleeper train to Inverness, then coach to Kirkaldy.

As there were ten family members, including Lilly, the Wardells had an entire sleeper carriage to themselves. Elisa's staff was travelling with them in a second public carriage.

The train rocked gently as Lilly moved forward along the narrow corridor, taking care to not snag her dress on any projections. The corridor was not made to accommodate crinolines.

The rhythmic clacking of the train wheels on the rail lines was soothing. She suspected she would be able to sleep tonight, perhaps even through the whole night—which was not always a given.

Jack and Will and Peter were in the lounge area. Jack helped himself to the brandy decanter, which rattled softly against the others inside the little brass fence used to hold them in place despite movements of the train.

Peter looked grumpy. He was only fifteen and grew bored easily.

Jack held the decanter up toward Lilly as she entered.

"No, thank you," she told him and sat next to Will. "Did Raymond miss the train, or is he travelling to Scotland later?"

Jack laughed softly and put the decanter back inside the fence.

"Is there something I should know?" Lilly asked, puzzled by Jack's reaction.

Will sat back, his arms along the top of the couch. The upholstered couch was a U shape and built against the wall of the carriage. "You didn't hear, then? Raymond is staying at Innesford House until the Great Family Gathering in October."

"Innesford…" Lilly looked down at her hands as the implications became clear.

"Do you still not believe us about Raymond and your mother, Lilly?" Jack asked, sitting on her other side.

Peter sat forward. "It all seems far too odd. Lilly's mother is…well, she's old!"

Will grinned. "Lady Natasha only seems old to you because you're still wet behind the ears."

Peter scowled. "Raymond is one of us. The cousins."

"Actually, he's thirty-three," Lilly said quietly. "The next oldest of the children in the Great Family is Benjamin. He is twenty-three. That is ten years' difference. Raymond has always been stranded in the middle, between us and our parents."

"Also, Benjamin is adopted, like me and Jack," Peter said.

"Jack and Patricia are not adopted," Will said. "They are fostered with us while their parents live in India." He said it with a tired, why-am-I-repeating-myself? tone, for Peter and the younger children always lumped Jack and Patricia in with them as having been adopted, for Jack and his sister had been living with Will's family since before anyone could remember.

Will turned back to Lilly. "Do you know how old your mother is?"

Lilly considered. She had never thought about her mother being any particular age. She had simply been there, a stable foundation in Lilly's life. "She sometimes spoke of my being born when she had barely turned twenty-one, so that would make her...just turned forty."

"Which is, of course, absolutely ancient, hey, Peter?" Jack teased.

Peter rolled his eyes.

Will put his lips together in a silent whistle. "There's only seven years' difference between her and Raymond. That makes it seem less odd than, say, Raymond taking up with you, Lilly. There's fourteen years between us and Raymond."

Jack tapped his fingernails against the brandy snifter. "When you put it that way, it doesn't seem completely unreasonable."

Will leaned forward. "The *ton* would lose their collective marbles over it, especially if there hasn't been a decent scandal lately, which there hasn't been."

"Why should they?" Lilly asked, indignation stirring.

Tracy Cooper-Posey

"Smooth your feathers, Lilly," Will said. "I only mean that with nothing else to snare their attention, everyone will focus upon your mother being older than Raymond and a widow, besides. Widows are supposed to decline and fade away, not have adventures with younger men."

"It is little wonder that everyone is being so guarded about this, even inside the family," Jack added.

Will shifted on the couch so he could see her face properly. "Do you mind, Lilly?"

"Isn't Cian the one you should be asking that?" Lilly replied. "He is the heir."

"Seth was your father, too."

Lilly flinched, yet managed not to let it show. "If Raymond and my mother really are forming some sort of... attachment, then I can't see I have any right to object."

The rest of her thoughts she did not speak aloud. Even if she had wild objections to the match, she would accept it, because she was in no position to judge morals or lack of them.

She deliberately moved the subject on, before Jack and Will asked the wrong questions. "Have you found out anything more about Susanna?"

Both men looked at her, Jack startled and Will with a thoughtful expression.

"Should we bother with all that now?" Jack asked. "If Raymond really has moved on…"

Lilly shook her head. "No. That is immaterial. We *must* find out who Susanna is."

"Why?" Will asked flatly. "You've been hounding us to

194

find Susanna for weeks and I've never really understood why you cared so much."

"Are you...fond of Raymond?" Jack asked.

"No," Lilly and Will said together.

"Not in that way," Lilly added.

"You and Raymond always have your heads together on family occasions," Jack pointed out.

"We are friends. Good friends," Lilly said defensively. "I am the oldest girl among the cousins. Raymond found it easier to talk to me, I suppose, than the younger cousins."

"He didn't see fit to tell you about your mother, though, did he?" Jack asked.

Lilly smiled. "Of course he didn't and for good reason. Raymond is far more discreet than both of you put together. He would not speak of...of affection for anyone else, until there was a match that could be announced publicly. In this case, he was twice as cautious because it is my mother who is involved. And besides," she added quickly, "no one in the family is really talking about it yet, are they?"

"We are," Will pointed out. "I guarantee the rumor will have travelled to Rhys and Annalies' family, too."

"Benjamin and Iefan are probably sighing with relief that their family is out of it for once," Jack added.

"How did we get back to Raymond and my mother, anyway?" Lilly complained. "We still need to find Susanna. Kirkaldy has a superior library. You and Will should go through the European peerage not included in *Burke's*. She may be there."

Will snorted. "Why on earth should we spend the opening of the hunting season locked up with dusty old books?"

"Because this is important, Will."

"Have you thought of simply asking Raymond who Susanna is?" Jack asked. "If you're so determined to uncover the woman, it might be best to go to the source, wouldn't it?"

"I *did* ask him, at last year's Gathering." She frowned. "He wouldn't tell me. He said her identity, if it were known, would threaten the family."

Jack considered that, his mouth pulled down.

"Instead, Raymond takes up with a far more unsuitable woman," Will finished. "Thereby threatening the family, anyway." As Lilly frowned, he added, "I speak, of course, only as the *ton* would see the affair. Personally, I don't give a damn. Raymond deserves whatever happiness he can carve out of life, after all he has been through."

"Listen to you, measuring propriety with a yard stick," Jack teased.

"It's a measure you should develop yourself, Jack," Will shot back. "We're both heirs to titles. After living with us for so many years, you still haven't learned how close our families—all our families—came to losing everything because of scandal?"

Jack considered Will, his gaze thoughtful. Then he sat back. "You may have a point."

"You're both missing the far larger point," Lilly said impatiently. "If Raymond will risk scandal by taking up with my mother, then how much greater must the risk to the family be if he won't speak of Susanna to anyone, even me?"

"The woman is long gone," Jack said tiredly. "With all due respect and humility, Lilly, I suggest you let it go."

"No," she said, frustration stirring. "I just want to protect the family, Jack. That includes you and Peter and Will and all the cousins. Everyone. She could still be a risk to us, only we won't know that until we know who she is. Do you not understand that I will do anything to preserve the family?"

Will tilted his head. "When did you become so concerned about the family? You couldn't see beyond the date of the next soiree, once."

Cold fingers walked up and down Lilly's spine, making her shiver. She had said far, far too much. Before she could say any more, she lurched to her feet and hurried from the lounge as fast as the swaying carriage would let her.

* * * * *

September and early October flew by far, far too fast, in Natasha's estimation. With the return of the staff and the family, Innesford House once more became the center of activity in the district. There was the official opening of the hunting season, held in Dunstall Woods, which lay on Innesford lands. There were hunting parties, riding parties and horse-racing events to attend and sometimes to officiate. The return of the families to their estates meant a round of calls to country houses to welcome everyone back.

When in Cornwall, Natasha naturally spent far more time with the children than she could manage in London, where engagements and at-homes were daily events. Here in the house, there were no neighbors to observe and disapprove of her mothering methods, or speak of her spoiling the children with her devotion.

The days fluttered past, most of them near perfect in their level of contentment and peace…and then there were the nights.

During the day, Raymond was a model houseguest. He was formally polite at both breakfast and dinner. He took his lunch in the small estate manager's office, which he had taken over in order to manage the Marblethorpe estate in Sussex, via a flurry of letters and written instructions. He was kind to the girls and friendly with Cian, the only boy home from either Eton or Cambridge. Somehow, Raymond had diffused the situation with Cian. He and Cian had returned from Truro that first day in a rented hack, with a horse from the Innesford stable tethered to the back of it. Cian had been outrageously drunk and Raymond had almost carried him to his old bedroom, while Natasha stripped away the dust covers and found a pillow for Cian's head.

She had spent a tense day, waiting for Cian to wake so they could deal with the unpleasantness. However, when Cian had walked carefully downstairs around sunset, he kissed her cheek as he always did and asked if he might have tea.

By then, Corcoran and the staff had arrived. The house was a chaotic swirl of people cleaning and packing away covers, while Cook exclaimed loudly in the kitchen over the mess left there.

Cian said nothing about Raymond and after a few days, Natasha relaxed. She had no idea what Raymond may have told her son. The two of them got on as well as they always had, even though Cian seemed wary when all three of them were in the same room at once. After a while, though, even Cian's tenseness disappeared, for Raymond did not so much as brush past her during the day.

The wild, tempestuous kisses they had risked in London did not happen here. There were no comments with double meanings, no risqué conversation. It meant that Natasha did not have to be on guard, monitoring what she said or how she behaved. She could remain as she always had been—a mother running a busy estate for her son, the Earl.

Instead, Raymond watched her. Sometimes, she would catch him observing her, with a guarded, brooding look that would disconcert her and make her think of a hawk circling above prey.

At other times, she would recognize the heat and speculation in his eyes for the passion it was. Often, when she saw that look in his eyes, she would forget what she had been saying and have to look away in order to marshal her thoughts once more. Or she would realize that she had frozen in the middle of some action—her embroidery needle held in mid-air, or the quoit she had been about to throw clenched in her hand while the twins complained about her inattention. Once, she had poured tea all over the tablecloth, ruining it forever, when she had forgotten she was in the processing of pouring a cup.

Raymond's heated looks would instantly turn her mind

to the promise of the night ahead and leave her to wander the house for the next few hours, unanchored and impatient.

The nights...oh, the nights!

At night, Raymond would come to her, sliding into her bed and wrapping his big body around her. He would hold her. Just hold her, as if he were making up for the day's lack. Their hands would stroke and slide and brush, travelling over places they had only traced with their eyes during the day. The stroking would turn to kisses, which would travel over the same places.

Natasha could bring herself to blushing just by thinking about what Raymond did to her and how much she enjoyed it. She had thought herself an experienced woman, however, Raymond was not simply experienced. He was inventive, curious and able to find sensitivities on her body that she was not aware she had.

The first time he had kissed her between her legs, she thought she would melt with a combination of mortification and delight, yet he had merely held her hips firmly in place and stroked her nub with his tongue until her pleasure peaked with almost painful intensity.

Her whole body was his to orchestrate and he was a thorough conductor. His explorations encouraged Natasha to experiment for herself. The first time she had thought to try kissing his shaft, he had directed her on the most effective way to manage it. His pleasure had been a distinct reward; he had shaken the bed with it, his hands gripping the rails until his knuckles whitened and the tendons straining in his neck.

When they were not busy with their hands and lips, they lay entwined and talked.

Those conversations were some of the most delightful she had ever had with anyone. Raymond was extremely well read and also thoughtful. "I have had a lifetime of reading and observation," he told her. "It has made me able to see things that others do not…or chose not to see."

He had always been a quiet man. Natasha had always assumed that his checkered beginnings in life—torn away from Elisa at a young age when the *ton* had presumed his mother had caused his father's murder by her promiscuous way, then shuffled from family member to family member, until Vaughn had rescued him—had left scars that made him stay cautiously silent and watchful. That was, until she had learned how deep his thoughts really ran.

Often they spoke of lighter things. Laughter, smothered and made quiet, frequently peppered their talk. Natasha enjoyed making Raymond laugh. Most often, he laughed about her tribulations, her daily challenges running a big household, and the vagaries of men who believed her incapable of putting together two coherent thoughts. Dealing with some of the local workers and artisans and farmers who thought it highly inappropriate to deal with a widow and a woman became less frustrating when she knew she could vent her irritation with Raymond, later.

October, and the week of the Great Family Gathering, drew near. Natasha fell to planning the week. This time, for this one occasion, she included both Raymond and Cian in the decisions and sometimes consulted the twins and Lisa Grace, on aspects that involved the children.

"It is an event for the whole family to enjoy," she told Raymond and Cian. "Therefore, the whole family can plan and execute it."

Corcoran and the household help were supplemented by local labor. The pavilion was unpacked, inspected, cleaned and prepared. The temporary tables for inside the pavilion were checked. The croquet sets, the cricket gear, and more balls, hoops and toys were assembled. The maze was given a close trim. The horses and ponies were groomed and prepared. Raymond and Corcoran walked down to the cliffs to closely examine the old wooden stairs down to the beach to ensure they were sound enough to support running feet, midnight adventures and more.

Mountains of food was prepared. The entire garden could not provide fresh produce for the twenty-eight people who would live and play together for a week, so local supplies were arranged and delivered in numerous carts and buggies. The sounds of industry and delicious smells drifted from the kitchen for days, as Cook made pies and cakes, biscuits and other delights and prepared to serve twenty-eight people at every meal.

Finally, the close of the Eton half arrived and with it, the start of the Gather. Because there was only one train running from Falmouth to Truro on the Sunday, everyone who was travelling to Cornwall arrived in Falmouth and waited there for the train to Truro. The arrival of everyone in Truro didn't always coordinate as precisely as Corcoran would wish. This year, though, it did. Everyone was on the same train, the four o'clock from Falmouth.

"They must very nearly fill the entire train," Cian said as they stood upon the platform, watching the steam rising from three miles away, as the train approached.

Corcoran was busy rounding up hacks to transport luggage and people back to the house. Even the Innesford charabanc could only carry twelve people—fewer, if their trunks came with them.

Cian moved down to the end of the platform, impatient for the train to arrive, while Natasha stood waiting toward the other end, where the first class carriages would stop.

Raymond came up to her side. His fingers tangled with hers, hidden inside a fold of her skirt.

Surprised, Natasha looked up at him. It was not like him to risk open affection. Not since London, at least.

"I regret the ending of this time," he murmured. "In all but one way, it has been perfect. Thank you for that."

"For the near perfection, or for ruining it with one flaw?" she asked, her heart thudding unhappily. She knew what the flaw was. It had remained unspoken for these past weeks.

Raymond's smile was small. Before he could answer, Corcoran came hurrying up to report on his success with the hacks and Raymond moved away, toward the bulletin board where the autumn fair was announced and the schedule for cathedral services had been pinned.

The train rounded the last gentle curve and was visible now, the chuffing louder.

Natasha stared at Raymond, her heart not calming. For one tiny moment, she had shared an intimacy with Raymond, right here in public, instead of hidden away in dark rooms and communicated by whispers. It had been... perfect.

Then the train was there, blowing steam and hissing noisily and doors were slid open with a bang. People stepped out onto the platform, dozens of them and not all of them part of the family. Those few hurried off the platform quickly.

The rest though, were chatting and laughing and calling to each other. The children immediately ran about the platform, chasing each other and working off the confinement they had suffered through the last few hours.

Porters with their trolleys wove among them all.

Natasha didn't move. She was frozen, her mind turning in faster and faster circles. Instead, she observed all the familiar faces, cataloguing the growth of the children over the last year, the changes in faces, fashion and appearances. Who was happy, who was discontented, who was yawning right there in public and had probably dozed on the train.

Lilly was there, wearing a sensible brown worsted suit, with her hair neat and tidy. Natasha's heart stirred. Poor Lilly...

Lilly saw Raymond and her face lit up. She hurried over to him, as close to a run as a lady could get and embraced him, right there for everyone to see. Lilly was not the only one doing that. Anna and Elisa were hugging Cian and talking happily, too.

Raymond hesitated for a moment, then hugged her back, his expression softening. They stood together, talking softly, in among the noisiest, largest family the station had ever seen.

The station master stood at the door to his little office, his arms crossed, as he watched the public spectacle. He did not look upset. The Innesford family was a part of Truro and the townsfolk were proud of them.

Vaughn moved over to Raymond and held out his hand. Rhys followed.

Raymond shook both hands, one after another and the three of them instantly fell to discussing something that could only be of interest to men, while Lilly stood quietly listening. Corcoran was bowing and nodding and trying to coax everyone to move toward the vehicles he had arranged for them. It was all so very, very normal.

An invisible band tightened around Natasha's chest, making it difficult to breathe, as she recognized the swirl of feelings in her breast. How long had she loved Raymond? She knew now, at last. She finally understood.

She had fallen in love with him.

"Oh, Seth..." she whispered, her eyes aching. She would not cry. Not here and not for this reason. She pulled her gaze away from Raymond, to give herself time to recover.

Morven Fortescue was standing at the end of the platform, right by the stairs down to the road, on the other side of the bulletin board from where everyone was standing and talking. She was carrying a small overnight bag and an umbrella and looked as though she had been about to descend the stairs, except that she was staring at Natasha. Her eyes were narrowed.

When Natasha saw her, Morven's expression shifted. It became wise. A small smile played about her lips.

Natasha barely felt any shock. The woman had a way of appearing wherever Natasha might be, with the most interesting timing. It seemed inevitable that at this, one of the most important moments of her life, the woman would be here to see it.

Natasha grabbed her skirt and petticoats and lifted them, so she could walk as swiftly as possible over to where Morven was standing. She stopped right in front of her. "For a lady who wishes only to retire to Scotland, you have an uncanny ability to arrive everywhere *but* Inverness."

Morven's face shifted again. She nodded. "I can understand why you might feel that way." She hefted the bag in her hand. "I have an establishment, not far away. I have come to finalize the sale of it, before returning to Inverness."

Natasha pulled her hands into fists. "Forgive my rudeness, but I do not believe you."

Morven gave a short laugh. "I finally speak a complete truth to you and it is the time you accuse me of lying."

"I beg your pardon?" Natasha said, confused.

Morven looked around. The happy noises on the other side of the platform were not abating. "I have a carriage, below," she said quickly. "We can talk there and no one will see you with me. Come along."

She turned to go.

"Why should I go anywhere with you?" Natasha asked.

Morven's blue eyes met hers. "I saw you looking at Marblethorpe just then. I recognize that look, Lady Innesford. I have seen it on countless faces. We must talk, you and I. You will find it to your benefit. Only, we must talk in my carriage. Believe me, you do not want to be seen with me here in Cornwall."

Natasha's heart fluttered uneasily. Morven did not wait for her response. She hurried down the steps, her sensible hoops swaying.

Natasha glanced around. Corcoran was still trying manfully to lead everyone to the carriages and the porters were still huffing as they moved trunks from the train. They would be busy for a while yet.

She turned and followed Morven Fortescue.

Chapter Fourteen

Vaughn and Rhys were arguing over the results of the stee-plechase at Newmarket when Raymond noticed Lilly edging away from the group in her silent way.

He caught her arm and pulled her to one side. "I apolo-gize. I forgot how you hate racing."

Lilly shook her head. "You belong with them more than you belong with me. Go back and talk."

"Now, what does that mean?" he asked.

Lilly's clear gaze met his. "I know about you and my mother, Raymond."

He let his surprise show. He could not help but glance around the platform, suddenly aware of their very public location.

"Oh, don't worry. No one outside the family knows," Lilly told him.

"How many *inside* the family know?" Raymond asked, his horror building.

"You have been at Innesford for two months. I would think everyone has made an assumption of some kind or another." She made to leave again.

"No, wait, please," he said quickly, trying to shrug off the concern she had just delivered. He would have to con-sider it later. "I wanted to ask you a question."

Lilly looked at him expectantly.

"It's just that…it may upset you."

"You have not done that already?" she asked.

Raymond shook his head. "It is important, Lilly. Could you…would you mind telling me how your father died?"

Her face grew pale and she stopped trying to pull her arm from his hand. "Why would you ask that?"

"I don't know how it happened. I thought I did. Now, I am not sure."

"Pneumonia," Lilly whispered. She wasn't even looking at him. "It came on fast and he went quickly."

Then she tugged at his hand again. Raymond let her go, his fingers nerveless.

* * * * *

Morven's carriage was plain and sensible, just as she was to outward appearances. The inside was warm enough. Natasha sat on the very edge of the seat opposite Morven, her uneasiness building, as Morven peered through the windows at the buildings of Truro, then lowered the blinds.

"Please hurry," Natasha said curtly. "I don't have much time."

Morven arranged her dress over her petticoats to her satisfaction, then put her hands on her lap and looked at Natasha. "Twenty-five years ago, my husband, Baronet Tachbrook, died. When he married me, I was a penniless commoner with a pretty face. After he died, I learned that he was as penniless as I. There were no children and all his family were dead, too. That was why there had been no opposition to his marriage to me. It left me with an estate with taxes due and a bare pantry."

Natasha stared at her. This was a story she had heard before. The misfortune of widows whose husbands could not manage their money were many. It also confirmed that Morven was as lonely as she had suspected and her pity grew.

"I made a decision," Morven said. "I moved from the northern end of the country all the way to the southern end."

"Cornwall," Natasha breathed.

"No one knew me here, of course. My husband had been insular and disinclined to travel. I could call myself anything I wanted here, so I took to using my middle name and earned my way by selling favors to gentlemen." Her gaze was direct. Uncompromising.

Natasha shrank back. "You are…are…" She couldn't speak the word. Horror was squeezing her throat.

"I *was* a prostitute," Morven said flatly. "I was a very good one. I built my own business and had half a dozen very high class women working for me. Gentlemen, especially those of rank, prefer the utmost discretion and I could give them that. It helped that I understood the challenges of their lives."

Natasha tried to breathe. Her stays were too tight. She desperately wanted to climb from the carriage and run all the way back to Innesford House. Her skin was crawling.

"Why are you telling me this?" she demanded of Morven.

"Raymond Devlin was a favorite client of mine, for more than ten years," Morven said.

Natasha moaned. She clutched at the door handle, illness making her weak and dizzy. "You lie," she whispered.

"Every year, Raymond would attend the family gathering at Innesford," Morven said. "Every year, I would visit him there, late at night. Why do you think he preferred the inferior accommodations of the carriage house? It was easier for me to slip in and out, there."

Natasha closed her eyes. Sound beat at her, muffling her hearing. It throbbed in her head.

"Are you listening, Lady Innesford?" Morven asked softly. Her voice sounded as though it was coming from a far distance.

Natasha shook her head. No. She would not listen to a moment more of this. Yet her hand had no strength to open the door.

"Even though I use the name Annette here, Raymond would call me Susanna," Morven said. "He insisted upon it."

Natasha drew in a hot, miasmic breath, shock giving her the strength to look at the creature sitting opposite her.

Morven nodded. "Yes, I thought that name might catch your attention." Her smile was soft. "It took me many years to realize that Raymond was desperately in love with the real Susanna and could not have her for some reason. I was the way he coped with not having her. I gave him a release he could find no other way."

Natasha couldn't speak. She could barely breathe. She could only stare helplessly at Morven as she said such dreadful things.

Morven was not gloating, though. She did not have a

vengeful glint in her eye. She even seemed to be a little sad. "Raymond refused to ever speak about Susanna, of course. You can imagine I was consumed by curiosity to know who had captured his heart so thoroughly. Then, last year, he did tell me."

"Who is she?" Natasha whispered. "That is why you pulled me in here, is it not? To tell me who she is?"

Morven nodded. "I saw your face, on the platform. You are in love with Raymond, only no one knows. I don't think Raymond knows, either."

Natasha swallowed. Of course he didn't know. She had just realized herself. Oh, of all the terrible moments for this woman to have seen her, it was that one!

Morven let out a frustrated hiss. "Susanna is *you*, Lady Innesford. Surely you must have suspected."

Natasha's heart creaked. "Me…? But…" It couldn't be. Her name wasn't Susanna, not even her middle name. If Raymond had loved her for more than ten years, then he would have been barely nineteen.

Her thoughts circled, faster and faster.

The carriage house. His isolation. The speculation among the family that Raymond was better than most men at hiding his indiscretions. In truth, he had never dabbled with a daughter of the peerage and lived to tell the tale. He had been in love with someone else—her—for ten years and had hidden it. Subsumed it, except for once a year, he had pretended this woman in front of Natasha, with her dark hair and blue eyes, was she.

"My name isn't Susanna," Natasha whispered. It was the

one hope she had that this awful revelation was wrong.

"You have forgotten your bible," Morven said complacently. "The Book of Daniel. Susanna was a married woman accused of meeting with a young man in her garden."

Natasha moaned sickly. It was true. It was all true. Raymond loved her—had *always* loved her. She fumbled for the latch and leaned on it. The door flung open under her weight and she stumbled out of the carriage into the mild light of late afternoon in October.

It was too bright. She held up her hand to shield her eyes and saw one of the local hackneys in front of her. Dazed, she stumbled over to it, fumbling with her reticule. She found a crown and held it up. It was too much. She didn't care.

The drive took the crown. "Innesford, my lady?"

Of course. Everyone knew who she was, here. She nodded and climbed mutely inside. The driver clicked the horses into motion and she clung to the back corner of the seat, ill with shock and shivering.

At last, she was at the house. She almost fell getting out of the cab and held on to the door until she was steady. Then she hurried into the house and called for Mulloy, who came running up from the kitchen, surprise on her face. "You're back, my lady? Where is everyone else?"

Natasha almost groaned again. Of course, the family would not be far behind. Corcoran would have nudged them into carriages by now.

She couldn't face them. Raymond would be among them and she desperately needed time to think.

"Pack my things, please, Mulloy," she told her maid. Her

lips weren't working properly. She removed her gloves and bonnet and gave them to her.

"Pack, my lady?" Mulloy asked, puzzled.

"I...I am returning to London at once." Although she had no idea what she would do there, except that it was away from Cornwall.

"But, my lady, everyone is *here,* aren't they?"

"Do what I ask, please," Natasha said stiffly. She looked around. She couldn't stay in the house. She couldn't be here when they returned. She moved through the house, leaving Mulloy gawping at her. Across the big drawing room and through the beautiful French doors, out onto the terrace. Her boots crunched on the gravel, then she was walking on lawn, freshly mowed and rolled in preparation for the gathering. She hurried. At the end of the lawn, which went for a very long way, there was a hedge with a gate. The gate was never locked, for all these lands, including the cliffs and the beach, belonged to the estate.

Natasha stepped through the gate, onto the wood slat path that led through the untamed countryside, to the very edge of the cliff. There, the path turned into steps that zigzagged down to the little cove beneath, with its turquoise waters and crescent beach. At the far eastern end of the bay was Innesford itself, the little village right on the promontory, with the harbor wall curving around protectively and the lighthouse at the end of it.

The wind was always strong here, throwing up enormous waves against the bluff at the other end of the cove. As Natasha started down the stairs, it wailed at her. Tendrils of hair whipped across her eyes. Above, gulls were hovering in the updraft, watching for fish.

She kept going. The keening of the wind matched the ache in her heart. This was where she needed to be.

By the time she reached the beach, though, the wind had dropped to an intermittent gust. It was only at the top of the cliffs that it had torn at her. Now, though, her hair was in disarray and hanging about her face. She unclipped it and shook it loose, then brushed her fingers through it. She picked up her skirt and headed over to the big pile of rocks. On the other side, the wind would be almost completely buffered and the very last of the daylight would warm the rock face.

The sand there was dry and soft. She tucked her skirt under her and settled on the sand itself, with her back against the rock, the fine wool of her skirt spread around her like a circus tent.

At last, she could think.

The only thought that would come to her was the overwhelming, astounding fact; she was Susanna. Raymond had loved her for years.

It occurred to her that perhaps Morven had lied about this, too. Except that it fit too neatly with everything that had puzzled her about Raymond. Nearly every question she had ever had was answered.

"Natasha."

She looked up, startled.

Raymond stood at the edge of the rocks. His hands were held in tight fists. His black eyes were narrowed with concern.

"How did you find me?" Natasha asked, dismayed.

"You left tracks in the sand." He pointed to the trail of deep boot prints in the damp sand in front of the rocks.

"Oh." She had forgotten about tracks. "I've never tried to run away before."

"Is that what you are doing? Mulloy babbled about going to London and that you looked as if you were sleep walking. It has taken me this long to find you…" He came a little closer.

It was there in her middle, squeezing the life out of her. She blurted it quickly, unable to stop. "I know who Susanna is."

Raymond grew absolutely still. Wariness touched his face. "You…know?"

"Annette has returned. She acquainted me with the truth."

He turned pale. His eyes cut away from her. He took a step, then another, as if he could not keep still, now. "You learn the truth and then you run away," he said softly. He closed his eyes and dropped his head. "I would have asked for just a little more time…" he whispered.

"Why didn't you tell me?" Natasha cried. "Why must I find out from *her*?"

He spun on his heels. "You have to ask that?" He threw out his hand. "I was *eighteen*, Natasha! You were married and so in love with your husband no one else existed. What was I supposed to do? Sing sonnets to you at your bedroom window?"

"You really…loved me, since then?" she asked, in a horrified whisper.

He lowered himself to one knee, the other tucked up against his chest, careless of the dark fabric of his trousers in the sand He looked at her. "Not at first," he admitted. "It was a simple crush then. Only it would not let me go. It just…*grew*," he ground out. "Every time I saw you, it grew a little more. Everything you did added to it. Your sweetness. Your love for everyone in your life. Your beauty…" His brow creased, as if he was in pain. "All other women were hags, compared to you."

Natasha lifted her knees up and hugged them over her skirt. She shivered. "I didn't know. I didn't even suspect."

"You weren't supposed to know," he said, his voice hoarse. "I hid it. I told no one. I knew how utterly hopeless it was, only I couldn't stop loving you. It built, every year. The idea of taking a wife…" He pounded his knee with his fist. "Well, I was brought to it at last. My father's family waged a campaign to bring me to the altar come hell or high water and they managed it at last, but it was a Pyrrhic victory. Rose got only a body. My soul and heart were yours and always would be." He uncurled his fist and looked at the mottled marks on his palm. "Then, when I had finally accepted my fate, Seth died."

Natasha's heart squeezed.

Raymond kept his gaze on his hand. "I knew I was being punished for my sin of loving a married woman. There I was, married myself, and you…" He shook his head. "I watched you cope. That first year without Seth, the strength you showed, to pick up all the pieces of his life and carry on, for Cian and your children. I couldn't tell you then, but my love for you almost consumed me. It was a bitter year, that year," he added softly.

Natasha closed her eyes. That year had passed almost trance-like. She had moved from one day to the next, doing what was needed, barely alive. Her children and their needs had pulled her through it.

"Then Rose died, giving birth to little Vaughn," he said. "I saw it as a sign that I was cursed to move through life alone. That was to be my fate."

"You didn't think to tell me, even then?" Natasha asked.

"Why would I do that?" he replied, looking at her. "You were in mourning. So was I—and I learned, I really *was* mourning Rose, in my way." He shook his head. "I would never have told you. I never intended to. Then, last June, I saw you at the cemetery, with tears on your cheeks." He turned his head away and his hand curled into fists again. "You know it all from there," he said heavily.

"Why not tell me when…when we kissed? Or when I saw you at Henley? There were so many times you might have spoken!"

"And said what, Natasha?" he asked, his tone reasonably. "Right at the moment when you were tentatively opening up your heart, braced for the world to hurt you again, waiting for *something* to go wrong and prove to you that you were wicked for even wanting to feel again…that was when I should have told you that I have obsessed about you for thirteen years and loved you for ten? You would have closed up like an oyster."

Natasha pressed her face against her knees. He was right. She would have been terrified to know that another man wanted her so badly. She was shaking with the knowledge even now. Yet it was different, now.

"Since June I have lived with the slenderest of hope," Raymond said. "I was so afraid that anything I did might snap that thread and snuff it for good. I had sleepless nights, wondering how I might get you to love me, if it was even possible—for you were a bud, opening up and it was *wondrous* to see."

Natasha lifted her head to look at him, startled.

He gave her a small smile. "Whatever happens now, that is one thing I will always be glad I could do for you. I helped you live again. Just as you helped me."

"You did do that," Natasha said softly.

He sighed. "I would have gone on waiting for you forever, as long as that hope remained alive." He dropped his head.

Natasha's eyes stung with the tears she had been holding at bay. "I do love you," she whispered.

Raymond jerked, as if she had struck him. His chin came up and his eyes glittered. "Yet you run away," he breathed, his chest rising and falling quickly.

"Because of Seth," she said. It hurt her throat to speak the words. "And now, because I know who Susanna is. Don't you see, Raymond? I thought we were a pair, you and I. I thought we had both lost someone we loved, only you never did lose Susanna. You never had her at all. Your love has remained constant and faithful. Your honor is unscathed, while I…I have fallen in love with another man. I've betrayed my love." She closed her eyes and hid her face again.

Raymond rested his hand on her shoulder. It was the lightest of touches. Even now, he was trying manfully not to influence her, to give her the time and room she needed to make up her own mind. "To love another doesn't take away from the first," he said softly. "You have demonstrated that your entire life. Your capacity for love is infinite. You loved Seth and every one of your children. You love your friends, every single one of their children, adopted strays and all. You pour your heart into your work with the Orphan Society. There is always room for more. One love does not take away the other."

Natasha lifted her head.

Raymond was right next to her, now, as close as he could get without stepping on her skirt. He was still accommodating, giving her room.

She drew in a shuddering breath. "Fight for me, Raymond, damn it. I don't want your understanding. I want you!"

He pulled her to him. "Say that again," he breathed, his voice strained.

"You've brought me this far," she whispered. "Take the last step. Don't leave me here."

His kiss almost crushed her. He pulled her against him and they both fell into the soft sand, so she was lying on top of him. Suddenly glad of the secluded corner of the cove that hid them, she rested over him as the kiss extended and deepened.

When he let her go, he wiped her cheeks, then brushed her hair over her shoulders. His gaze met hers. "Marry me," he said, his voice low. It rumbled against her torso, too.

"Is that a demand?" she asked, delighted.

"Yes, damn it."

"Then yes, I will marry you." She hesitated. "Only… perhaps we should tell the children, first? And…oh, lord, Elisa and Anna and Vaughn and Rhys, they're back at the house, my God…" She tried to rise.

Raymond held her down easily. "They will wait for a few more minutes," he told her. "Take some time for yourself, first."

She relaxed against him.

Raymond cupped her face. "I love you. With every breath I take, I love you."

Natasha shivered. "And I love you." She rested her cheek against his shoulder. "And I am happy!" she said wonderingly. "This could not be a less romantic spot for a proposal, except I am wildly happy anyway."

Raymond turned his head to look at the waves and the gulls above. "This is the perfect place," he said. "This is where it all started."

She looked at him. "Started?"

"This is where I saw you for the first time as a woman and desirable." He laughed and sat up, bringing her with him. "You don't know. Of course you don't. Do you know why I called you Susanna?" He pushed her hair back again, as the breeze caught it.

"Because of the story in the bible," she said. "That woman told me."

"Well, then." He laughed.

"I don't understand. What has this place to do with it?"

"The very first Family Gathering," he told her. "I was eighteen and I used the carriage house because I didn't want to sleep with the children in the dormitory."

"I remember," Natasha said, frowning.

He kissed her briefly. "Do you remember Seth stealing you across the garden in the night, with you wearing naught but your nightdress?"

Natasha drew in a sharp, shocked breath. "Oh my lord!" She covered her mouth. "We came down here." She looked around. "The house was full of people and Seth was feeling hemmed in. We came down here to breathe salt air and…" Her cheeks burned. "We swam in the ocean."

Raymond nodded. "Naked."

"You *watched*!"

"I could not stop watching. I couldn't make myself look away. I stayed up there." He lifted his chin to indicate the cliff tops. "That was the start of it for me. I had noticed you as a woman and I not go back to thinking of you as my honorary aunt after that."

"You stopped calling me Aunt Natasha years ago," she agreed.

"That was the year I stopped," he said gently and kissed her. "And the year I started to love you, instead."

Chapter Fifteen

Everyone except the smallest children was in the drawing room. Corcoran was busy filling snifters and passing out cups of tea.

As Natasha and Raymond stepped into the drawing room through the French doors, she could hear the younger children upstairs, stomping and yelling in sheer exuberance. The first night of a gathering was always an energetic one.

Annalies hurried over to them. "There you are!" she said. "Mulloy was making no sense, talking about London and ghosts. You were on the beach?"

Elisa moved around Natasha, appraising her critically. "You have sand all *over* you," she added.

Vaughn came up to Raymond's side and brushed at the shoulder of his jacket. "So do you," he said.

Raymond nodded. He held out his hand to her and Natasha took it. Her heart hammered.

"Everyone, I would like you to meet my Susanna," Raymond said.

The silence stretched for too many hard beats of her heart. Natasha watched Elisa, her breath suspended.

Annalies drew in a sharp breath, her hands pressed together, a smile forming. She did not speak, though. Her gaze flicked toward Elisa and Vaughn.

It was Will who broke the silence. He groaned, holding

his head. "The Book of Daniel! I missed it completely!"

Jack frowned. "Isn't that about a nude woman in a garden?"

Will shoved his elbow in Jack's ribs, silencing him.

Vaughn let out a gusty breath. "Well…"

Raymond squeezed Natasha's hand even tighter. "We will be married as fast as we can arrange it. I would prefer tonight, only Natasha says tomorrow at the earliest."

"Nonsense," Elisa said firmly. "You can't possibly be married before the end of the week. We have a dress to see to and a wedding breakfast." Yet her eyes were glittering with tears as she spoke.

Natasha let go of Raymond's hand and hugged her.

Elisa clung to her, her normal sense of decency abandoned. Natasha could feel her shoulders shaking. Annalies patted Elisa's back, biting her own lip.

"I think champagne is in order, Corcoran," Rhys said softly.

"I believe so, sir," Corcoran said and hurried off.

Elisa stepped back and straightened her dress and cleared her throat, then dashed her eyes with the back of her hand. "I *am* happy for you. Both of you. I don't understand why I did that."

Vaughn took her in his arms and she hid her face against his shoulder.

Rhys rested his hand on Raymond's shoulder. "You don't want to wait? Call bans and formalize it?"

"The way you did?" Raymond asked him bluntly.

"Ah, well." Rhys took Annalies' hand. "None of us is a

good example to follow."

Raymond shook his hand and picked up Natasha's hand again. "A quiet wedding, as fast as possible. No more waiting." Then, in front of everyone, he turned to her and kissed her.

Chapter Sixteen

Raymond found her in the formal garden behind the maze, sometime after the last of the family had left for Truro and the train. He took Natasha in his arms and kissed her soundly.

Natasha was happy to be kissed, right there in the open.

"Hello, Mrs. Devlin," he murmured against her lips. "Are you hiding out here?"

"Enjoying the silence, Mr. Devlin," she admitted. "It has been a very noisy week."

"Gathers usually are noisy. This one was much louder than usual." He turned, bringing her with him, his arm around her, to see what she had been doing. "Very domestic," he observed. "Does Henty not prune the roses for you?"

"He does," Natasha admitted. "However, this particular bush seems to only respond to me. Henty near killed it for three years before I took over. He says it's actually something in the soil here—the limestone—that makes it grow, only he's just superstitious enough to ask me to cut it back before the frost." She sighed. "It bloomed for the first time, the year Seth died."

Raymond took her hand and walked around the bush. "There's a bloom here you missed…" Then he straightened up with a snap. "It's black," he said quietly.

Natasha laughed self-consciously. "Seth had it brought

back from Turkey one year. It's only supposed to grow there. He wanted to try, anyway."

Raymond took the sheers from her hand and put them down, then took both her hands in his. "You were the one who sent me the ebony roses, when Rose died."

Natasha jumped a little. "Yes, I did," she admitted. "It seems so silly now. I wanted to let you know I knew exactly what you were going through. At the same time, I didn't want to bother you while you were grieving."

"You cared," Raymond said, his voice low. "All along, you did care."

"Of course I did," she said warmly. "You are family."

"Those roses were what made me come here, last year. I had withdrawn from everything, almost to the bitter end. The roses told me that there might possibly be something worth living for, somewhere." He laughed. "And there was."

He kissed her and Natasha let herself melt into her husband's arms, regardless of who might be watching.

Did you enjoy this book?

How to make a big difference!

Reviews are *powerful*.

Authors like me, without the financial muscle of a sleek New York publisher backing me, can't take advertisements out in the subways and billboards of the world.

On the other hand, New York publishers would *kill* to get what I have: A committed and loyal group of readers.

Honest reviews of my books help bring them to the attention of other readers. If you enjoyed this book I would be grateful if you could spend just a few minutes leaving a review (it can be as short as you like) on the book's page where you bought it.

Thank you so much!

Tracy

The next book in the

Scandalous Scions series.

The next book in this series will be released in October 2017. In the meantime, have you read the original Scandalous Sirens series?

Forbidden, Book 1, Scandalous Sirens

By J.A. Templeton and Tracy Cooper-Posey

Vaughn wants revenge. Elisa wants her son back. Neither expected to want each other.

Elisa's determined to have her son back at any cost, even if it means marrying a vicious stoat of a man like Rufus Wardell, but her plans and her life are turned upside down by the sudden reappearance of Rufus' grown and estranged son, Vaughn.

Lured by the contrast of Elisa's sweet beauty with the wicked rumors of her wanton past, Vaughn embarks on a seduction as scorching as it is daring. What he finds is not at all what he sought: Elisa is an innocent, but with a sensuality so raw he cannot resist her…

…even though their passion is forbidden.

Amazon #1 Best Seller, Historical Romance
ARE Bestseller, Historical Romance

Amazon Best Seller, Regency Romances
CAPA Award Finalist

The wonderful end **deserves cheers**. —Sensual Romance

About the Author

Tracy Cooper-Posey is an Amazon #1 Best Selling Author. She writes science fiction and romance. She has published over 90 books since 1999, been nominated for five CAPAs including Favorite Author, and won the Emma Darcy Award.

She turned to indie publishing in 2011. Her indie titles have been nominated four times for Book Of The Year and *Byzantine Heartbreak* was a 2012 winner. *Faring Soul* won a SFR Galaxy Award in 2016 for "Most Intriguing Philosophical/Social Science Questions in Galaxybuilding" She has been a national magazine editor and for a decade she taught writing at MacEwan University.

She is addicted to Irish Breakfast tea and chocolate, sometimes taken together. In her spare time she enjoys history, Sherlock Holmes, reading science fiction and ignoring her treadmill. An Australian Canadian, she lives in Edmonton, Canada with her husband, a former professional wrestler, where she moved in 1996 after meeting him on-line.

Other books by

Tracy Cooper-Posey

For reviews, excerpts, and more about each title, visit Tracy's site and click on the cover you are interested in: http://tracycooperposey.com/books-by-thumbnail/

* = ebook version is free!

Blood Knot Series
(Urban Fantasy Paranormal Series)
Blood Knot*
Southampton Swindle
Broken Promise
Vale
Amor Meus
Blood Stone
Blood Unleashed
Blood Drive
Blood Revealed
Blood Ascendant

Beloved Bloody Time Series
(Paranormal Futuristic Time Travel)
Bannockburn Binding*
Wait
Byzantine Heartbreak
Viennese Agreement
Romani Armada
Spartan Resistance
Celtic Crossing

Kiss Across Time Series

(Paranormal Time Travel)
Kiss Across Time*
Kiss Across Swords
Time Kissed Moments I
Kiss Across Chains
Kiss Across Deserts
Kiss Across Kingdoms
Time and Tyra Again
Kiss Across Seas
Kiss Across Worlds

The Kine Prophecies

(Epic Norse Fantasy Romance)
The Branded Rose Prophecy

The Stonebrood Saga

(Gargoyle Paranormal Series)
Carson's Night*
Beauty's Beasts
Harvest of Holidays
Unbearable
Sabrina's Clan
Pay the Ferryman
Hearts of Stone

Destiny's Trinities

(Urban Fantasy Romance Series)
Beth's Acceptance*
Mia's Return
Sera's Gift
The First Trinity (Stories 1-3)
Cora's Secret
Zoe's Blockade
Octavia's War
The Second Trinity (Stories 4-6)
Terra's Victory
Destiny's Trinities (Series Box)

Interspace Origins
(Science Fiction Romance Series)
Faring Soul
Varkan Rise
Cat and Company
Interspace Origins (Series Box)

Short Paranormals
Solstice Surrender
Eva's Last Dance
Three Taps, Then….
The Well of Rnomath

The Vistaria Affair
(Romantic Suspense)
Red Leopard*
Black Heart
Blue Knight
White Dawn

Go-get-'em Women
(Short Romantic Suspense Series)
The Royal Talisman
Delly's Last Night
Vivian's Return
Ningaloo Nights

The Endurance
(Science Fiction Romance Series)
5,001
Greyson's Doom
Yesterday's Legacy
Promissory Note
Quiver and Crave
Xenogenesis
Junkyard Heroes
Evangeliya
Skinwalker's Bane

Scandalous Sirens

(Historical Romance Series)
Forbidden*
Dangerous Beauty
Perilous Princess

Scandalous Scions

(Historical Romance Spin Off)
Rose of Ebony
Soul of Sin

Romantic Thrillers Series

Fatal Wild Child
Dead Again
Dead Double
Terror Stash
Thrilling Affair (Boxed Set)

Jewells of Tomorrow

(Historical Romantic Suspense)
Diana By The Moon
Heart of Vengeance

Contemporary Romances

Lucifer's Lover
An Inconvenient Lover

The Sherlock Holmes Series

(Romantic Suspense/Mystery)
Chronicles of the Lost Years
The Case of the Reluctant Agent
Sherlock Boxed In

The Indigo Reports
(*Space Opera*)
Flying Blind
New Star Rising
But Now I See
Stars Eclipsed
Worlds Beyond

Non Fiction Titles

Reading Order
(*Non-Fiction, Reference*)
Reading Order 2016

CPSIA information can be obtained
at www.ICGtesting.com
Printed in the USA
LVHW082324071222
734804LV00038B/1773

9 781772 632828